Double the Danger

One of the men caught my eye. His jaw tightened, and he said something to the two men with him.

"We've been spotted," I told Frank. "And they know we know they know."

Frank gave me a confused look. "Uh, I think I understood that."

The three men spun around and faded into the crowd.

"I want to know what they're up to," I said.

"Right behind you, bro," said Frank.

We sprinted after them. They hurried around a corner, and we picked up speed. We didn't want to lose them.

My heart nearly jumped out of my chest as a car screeched to a sudden stop just inches from me. Squealing tires and honking horns shrieked around us as we darted between yellow taxis. As I rounded the next corner, I saw the three goons vanish into a limo. Frank dashed up beside me.

"They're in that car," I told him.

"You mean the one headed straight for us?" asked Frank. "Jump!"

THE HARDY BOYS

Undercover Brothers®

Available from Simon & Schuster

THE HARDY BOYS

Undercover Brothers®

BOYS

FRANKLIN W. DIXON

#27 Double Deception

Aladdin Paperbacks

New York   London   Toronto   Sydney

ALADDIN PAPERBACKS
An imprint of Simon & Schuster Children's Publishing Division
1230 Avenue of the Americas, New York, NY 10020
Copyright © 2009 by Simon & Schuster, Inc.
All rights reserved, including the right of reproduction in whole or in part in any form.
THE HARDY BOYS MYSTERY STORIES is a trademark of Simon & Schuster, Inc.
ALADDIN PAPERBACKS, HARDY BOYS UNDERCOVER BROTHERS, and related logos are registered trademarks of Simon & Schuster, Inc.
Designed by Sammy Yuen Jr.
The text of this book was set in Aldine 401 BT.
Manufactured in the United States of America
First Aladdin Paperbacks edition March 2009
10 9 8 7 6 5 4 3 2 1
Library of Congress Control Number 2008037934
ISBN-13: 978-1-4169-6766-8
ISBN-10: 1-4169-6766-4

TABLE OF CONTENTS

Where's Ryan?

Things have a way of happening around teen movie star Justin Carraway. Crazy things, fun things, surprising things. But also some pretty scary, deadly, and *nearly* deadly things.

My brother Joe and I take that all in stride. After all, we're part of American Teens Against Crime—ATAC—and it's all part of the gig.

Like tonight.

In short order we found Justin's longtime manager, John "Slick" Slickstein , murdered, linked him to the bootleg DVD ring operating in Atlantic City and China, identified Phillip Yu as the head of the crime syndicate, and had the harrowing experience of fighting the martial arts expert in a spiraling helicopter!

Phillip lost that fight. Actually, he bailed. He leaped out of the helicopter and into the churning Atlantic Ocean below us.

Quite a day's work.

And now, well after midnight, it still wasn't over. We were in the deserted Steel Pier amusement park in Atlantic City, where we had just landed the helicopter Phillip had stolen. It was deserted, except for the cops we had called and the EMTs who turn up at these things. The police were asking questions. Justin was pacing a few yards away, trying to keep his very recognizable face hidden. Then, in the middle of all the craziness, Rick Ortiz, the head production assistant on Justin's film crew, showed up, looking scared. He announced that Justin's twin brother might have just been swept away in a terrible hurricane.

Never a dull moment.

Ryan Carraway took off about a week ago without a word to anyone. Justin said his twin went to Isola, a little Caribbean island, for some well-deserved R & R. One problem: Isola lies smack in the path of that hurricane I mentioned.

This news was very confusing, though. See, right before the fight on the helicopter, we'd run into Justin on the boardwalk. He told us he'd just been talking to Ryan on his cell, telling him about Slick's murder. No mention of a devastating storm.

"The storm hit two days ago," Rick explained, equally confused. "There's been no service at all!"

"If Ryan is still on that island, we know people who can help," I said.

"And if he's not?" asked Rick, obviously very worried.

"We should track him down anyway," Joe said. "With all that's happened here, I'm sure Ryan would want to be with Justin."

"True," I said. "After losing Slick, they need each other."

Slick Slickstein had taken over as Justin and Ryan's manager after he discovered their own father was stealing from them. Harsh, right? He stepped in as more than a manager. He was really like a father figure. Or so we thought. Turns out, Slick was just as crooked. But we hadn't told Justin or Ryan that. It just seemed too soon.

With Ryan gone, Justin was having to deal with a lot of heavy stuff on his own.

Though if I were Ryan, I probably would have split a long time ago. Living in Justin's shadow, working for him, cleaning up the messes he makes . . . well, let's just say, if I had to do that for Joe? Don't even go there.

I imagine the hardest part is that they both started

out famous. As little kids they shared a role on a popular TV show. They do that with child actors. Kids aren't allowed to work too many hours a day. So they hire twins—sometimes even triplets—and swap them out. But once the boys got older, Slick decided that only one of them could get really famous. He decided Justin was the one.

We first met Justin and Ryan because of a mission for ATAC, tracking down a dangerous stalker who had targeted Justin. We were able to get into the Justin orbit so easily because he requires so much minding. You know that saying "It takes a village to raise a child"? Well, it takes more like a whole *nation* to keep track of Justin.

When Ryan took off, Rick the PA and Sydney Lamb the publicist both asked us to stick around to pick up the slack. We jumped at the chance—partly because, well, it was fun, but also because we just didn't feel like the murder of paparazzi Elijah Gorman had been solved. Then, while we were in Atlantic City, ATAC asked us to look into an illegal film distribution ring, which was flooding the Chinese market with Justin Carraway flicks.

Now that we'd finished up that case, it looked like we had another. Finding and possibly rescuing Ryan Carraway.

"Justin," I told the seventeen-year-old megastar,

"we promise we'll take care of this. We'll find Ryan and make sure he's okay."

"He's fine," Justin said. "I told you—I just spoke to him."

Rick stared at Justin, completely bewildered. "But how is that possible? On the news—"

Justin cut him off. "Look, maybe Ryan had already left the island. He was using a cell. As in *mobile*. He could be anywhere. Obviously, wherever he was, there wasn't a hurricane."

"But why wouldn't he tell you if he left Isola?" Rick pressed.

"Maybe because I had just told him that Slick—a guy we've known since we were little kids—was murdered. It just didn't come up, okay?"

I could see Rick had pushed him too far. And Justin had a point. When you give news like that to someone, it's not like you get around to other things.

"Listen," I said, not wanting to upset Justin further. "It's late, a lot has happened. Let's just call it a night."

The next morning we headed back to Bayport. While we were in Atlantic City, the filming of Justin's next movie, *Undercover*, had continued. The second unit had stayed behind and shot the scenes Justin wasn't in.

JOE

Listen to the filmmaking expert. "Second unit." Excuse me, Mr. Spielberg.

FRANK

Whatever. Just because I actually bothered to learn the correct terms . . .

Anyway, as I was saying. The minute we arrived home, Aunt Trudy corralled us into the kitchen. I'm as big on snacks as the next guy, but I knew what she was up to. She wasn't plying us with chocolaty goodness because she loves us. No, this was chocolate bribery. She was after stories about Justin.

"So what did he wear?" Aunt T asked, loading my plate with freshly baked chocolate brownies.

I know I've said this before, but it bears repeating. My aunt's crush on Justin is more than a little weird. She thinks he has *charisma*. She's even bought memorabilia from his website, Justin Time.

"Wear?" Joe repeated, taking a thoughtful munch of the still warm brownie. "Gee, I can't really remember. Maybe a glass of milk would help."

Aunt Trudy dropped the brownie pan and poured two big glasses of milk.

Hmm. This could come in handy. Dangle Justin

tidbits as barter. *No*, I scolded myself. *That's no way to treat Aunt T.*

Joe gulped his milk. "A tux. In the casino scene, Justin wore a tux."

Aunt T's eyes got a little dreamy. "He'd look good in a tux."

I'd heard enough. "I'm going to go unpack."

"We also went surfing with him," Joe was saying as I left the room. "Hey, can I get this brownie à la mode?"

I shook my head as I went into my room. I had just dropped my backpack when my dad walked in. He shut the door behind him, so I knew he wanted to talk about the mission.

Dad's the only one in the family who knows that Joe and I are part of ATAC. In fact, we were Dad's first recruits. He created ATAC for those cases where a teenager would have an easier time getting information. Like with Justin. Would he want some boring, buzz-killing adult hanging around as part of his entourage? No. He'd want a coupla cool dudes like me and Joe. We'd get the real deal, not the act put on for the parent-types.

"Congratulations," Dad said. "Job well done."

"Thanks. Listen, something came up that I think your contacts can help with."

"What's that?"

"Justin's twin brother Ryan was on Isola in the Caribbean. Right in the path of that hurricane. But Justin was talking to him right after. Can you try to find out where he might have been evacuated to?"

"That shouldn't be a problem."

"Everyone would feel a lot better knowing that Ryan's okay. Rick wants him to know the whole crew misses him."

"No kidding, Rick misses him," said Joe, strolling into the room.

"Knock, ever?" I asked.

Joe shrugged. "Whatever. Anyway, Rick misses Ryan because Ryan did a whole lot of Justin management. Now it all falls to him."

"And us," I pointed out. "That's why we're still working as assistants."

"I'll see what I can find out," Dad said. "Glad you're back. In one piece." He left the room and closed the door.

Joe grabbed a tennis ball, sprawled on my bed, and started bouncing the ball against the wall.

"Something's weird here," he said.

"Your Spidey sense tingling, bro?" I asked.

"Not exactly. Just, I don't know. . . . Closing this case feels like winning a match on a decision rather than a knockout punch."

"I hear you," I said. "Phillip's jump into the ocean

meant we didn't get to bring him to justice."

"Or tie up all the loose ends."

"Like the dead paparazzo." I nodded. "Like how the bootleg ring worked. We didn't even get to wipe that smirk off Phillip Yu's face."

"Yeah, I think that's the part that bugs me most," Joe admitted.

There was a knock on the door.

"You see?" I told Joe. "That's how human beings enter rooms."

"Ha, ha." He bounced the ball again.

"Come in," I called.

Our dad walked in with his phone. "Here," he said, handing it to me. "I've got one of my contacts on the line. She already knows the situation and has some information."

"What did you find out?" I said into the phone.

"As you know," the woman on the other end of the line said, "there was a terrible hurricane. There are—were—three hotels on the island, and everyone has been accounted for. But your friend Ryan Carraway was never registered at any of them."

I blinked a few times. This didn't make any sense. "Are you sure?" Then I remembered something we'd only recently discovered. "He might have checked in under a different name. Try Ziziska. That's his *real* name." I spelled it for her.

"I don't think we'll find anything, but I'll check," she said. I heard clicking, and I figured she was typing into a computer. "No. No Ziziska."

"He could be using a made-up name," I suggested.

"Not likely. You see, we didn't just check the names in the registers, we used his photo. No one matching his description ever checked in. Anywhere."

"Well, thanks for looking into it." I handed Dad back his phone. I told them what the woman had said.

"He must never have been there," Joe said. "He looks *exactly* like Justin. If he had been on that island, *someone* would have noticed him. Isola isn't your typical tourist trap, but it's not on the moon."

"So what's going on?" I asked. "Did Justin lie about where Ryan went—or did Ryan lie to Justin?"

"I think we have a mystery on our hands," said Joe.

"And I have a feeling you boys are determined to get to the bottom of it," Dad said.

He was right about that.

Straight to the Source

"I say we go straight to the source," I suggested as we all left Frank's room. "We'll ask Justin."

"We know where to find him," said Frank. "We're supposed to be back at the set in a few."

"Let me know if you need anything else," said Dad.

"Will do," I told him. He vanished into the kitchen. If he was hoping for brownies, well . . . let's just say the Justin card is very effective. There weren't any left.

We opened the front door and discovered our mom carrying shopping bags and her briefcase.

"Going out again already?" she asked. "You just got home!"

Frank grabbed one of the shopping bags from her. "Sorry, but they're shooting tonight." I took the other bag, and we carried them into the kitchen.

"But I haven't even seen you!" Mom complained.

"It's a job, remember?" I said. "We have to stick to our commitments. Right?"

"I guess I can't argue with that," said Mom with a sigh. "But do you always have to miss dinner?"

"Don't worry," I said, with a wink to Aunt Trudy. "Aunt T took care of us already."

The sun was low on the horizon as we rode our motorcycles to the deserted area on the docks serving as the set that night.

Trailers were parked along one block. These were where the actors hung out when they weren't needed. I noticed another trailer was being used for costumes, and still another seemed to have been set up as an office.

A very pretty girl with long blond hair and green eyes came out of one of the trailers. Justin's costar, Emily Slater.

"Hi, Emily," I called.

She frowned slightly, as if she was trying to place me. "Oh, hi," she said, coming over to join Frank and me. "So you're still hanging around the dillweed?"

That was our special name for Justin. As you probably guessed, she's not a fan. We briefly bonded over that fact.

"Actually, we're working," said Frank. "We got hired on to help Rick Ortiz, since Ryan isn't around."

"Unbelievable Ryan just bailed like that," she said. Then she smirked. "Good for him. I can't believe how much he took from Justin."

"Have you heard from Ryan?"

Emily shook her head. "Nope. No one has." She ran a hand through her long hair. "I have to get into hair and makeup." She grimaced. "It will take all my best acting skills to act as if I'm totally in love with Justin."

"You'll do great," I said. "You always do."

I watched Emily walk away. Frank punched my arm.

"What?" I asked, rubbing the spot where he hit me.

"So out of your league," he teased.

"A guy can dream, can't he?"

A trailer door slammed and Justin strode toward us, head down. He would have slammed right into me if I hadn't quickly stepped out of his way.

"Yo, dude," I said. "Lose something?"

"Huh?" Justin stared at me.

"I thought you might have dropped something, the way you're staring down at the ground."

"What? Oh. No." He shoved his hands into his pockets and rocked on his heels. "You two still doing the assistant thing?"

"We're about to check in with Rick," Frank told him.

"Yeah. Good. Well, see you." Justin stalked away.

Frank and I were quiet for a moment. "Is it just me," I said finally, "or was Justin a whole lot less friendly than usual?"

"Not just you. But I don't think it's us. He seems worried about something."

"Ryan, maybe?" I suggested.

I watched Justin as he headed over to the set. Emily Slater noticed him approaching and deliberately turned her back on him. Justin stared at her back for a minute, then slunk away to the food table.

"I wonder if the director will get through the scenes without them having some kind of fight," I said.

"Maybe that's what has Justin so preoccupied," Frank suggested. "He had a few days away from dealing with Emily when we were in Atlantic City. Now he has to work with her again."

"There's Rick," I said, pointing out the dark-haired production assistant. He was talking to

Sydney Lamb, Justin's publicist. She wore the most amazing outfits—and I don't necessarily mean that in a good way. Today she resembled an alien from a sci-fi flick, with a kind of silvery tunic over leggings, long silver mesh gloves, and dark glasses, even though there was barely any light left.

"Hello, darlings!" Sydney gave us each air kisses when we joined them. Why do Hollywood people do that?

"I'd like you guys on crowd control," said Rick. "It shouldn't be too bad in this location, but there are bound to be gawkers. We want to be sure no one walks through any of the shots."

"Will do," Frank said.

Justin came over. "Why aren't there more cops?" he demanded.

I scanned the area. As usual, whenever a film is shooting on city streets, there were several police around, as well as patrol cars blocking off the alley so that no one could drive in.

"I think we're covered," Rick said.

"Well, I *don't* think we're covered," Justin snapped. "So do something about it,"

Rick looked startled, then said, "Of course." He disappeared into the office.

"He already asked us to help with crowd control," I assured Justin.

Justin eyed us up and down. "No offense, guys. I know you've done a lot of really brave things and can hold your own. But I'd still feel a lot safer with more uniforms." He turned and went back to his trailer. He glanced Emily's way, and once again she very obviously ignored him.

Weird. Security wasn't usually something Justin worried about. He was more concerned with making sure he could get away from the people who were trying to look out for him.

Sydney sighed. "I'm worried about that boy. I'm sure Slick's murder is hitting him a lot harder than he's letting on."

Frank and I exchanged a look, silently agreeing to keep quiet. No one but ATAC knew about Slick's role in the bootlegging scheme. Phillip Yu had needed an industry insider—someone who would have access to the original films so that he could make high-quality copies. Slick not only had an advance DVD of *Hong Kong Challenge*, Justin's movie that was about to premiere, he also had one of the bootleg versions.

It seemed too soon to tell Justin that a guy he'd trusted all his life was stealing from him. He'd find out soon enough. Besides, until they were able to make arrests, the authorities didn't want any of the details revealed.

"I wish Ryan were around," Sydney said. "And not just because I now have to do the tasks he usually took care of."

"Have you heard from him?" I asked.

"Not a peep. Justin said he wanted a total break, so I'm respecting that. But I do plan to wring his neck when he comes back. He's the *good* twin! How could he leave me with the *evil* one?" She smiled as she said it, so I knew she was kidding. She truly cared about both Ryan and Justin.

"I have to double-check the shooting schedule," she said. "Justin needs to be available for some appearances. Ciao!"

She clicked away on her high heels into the trailer office.

"Why do you think Justin is so worried about security?" I asked.

"Maybe it's a reaction to Slick's murder," Frank suggested. "If a guy close to me got whacked, it would definitely have me looking over my shoulder."

"Good point."

"Hey, we never talked to Justin about Ryan," I remembered.

"They're still fiddling with the lights," said Frank. "It doesn't look like they're going to be starting any time soon. Now's good."

We walked over to his trailer and knocked on the door.

"Enter!" he said.

We stepped through the door. These trailers weren't very tricked out, since they were rentals being used for only a few days and weren't intended for sleeping. Justin's had a table, a small sofa, and a few chairs. A mirror ran along one wall, with a counter he could use for makeup, I guessed, but he had a game console set up instead. There was also a tiny kitchenette and a door leading to the bathroom, and that was it.

Justin was sitting on the sofa, looking at his script. I dropped onto the arm of his couch, and Frank hovered in the doorway. Three guys, each over six feet tall, and this space got crowded.

"Listen, we just wanted to let you know that Ryan isn't on Isola," I said.

Justin never looked up. "I told you he was fine."

"The thing is, it looks as if he was never there," said Frank.

Now we had gotten his attention. "What do you mean?"

"Our friends," I explained, "actually know that island pretty well. No one matching Ryan's description has been seen, and he never checked into any of the hotels."

"You went to a lot of trouble," Justin said. "I told you not to bother."

"We like Ryan," said Frank. "People are worried about him. If he was evacuated somewhere, we want to help."

"How could you help?" Justin asked. "You're just high school kids in Bayport. Oh, right . . . you *know* people."

I couldn't tell if he was skeptical or suspicious, but we were entering dangerous territory here. "Our mom—she went to school with someone who has a vacation house there," I said.

I hoped he bought it. It did look kind of strange for two high school kids to have the resources to track people down in foreign countries!

"Look. If Ryan didn't want anyone to know where he went, that's his own business." Justin shrugged. "So he went somewhere else. No biggie."

"I guess. . . ."

Justin seemed weirdly unconcerned. I got the sense he actually knew where Ryan was, he just wasn't telling.

Someone knocked on the door. "They're ready on the set," a voice on the other side of the door announced.

"Gotta go, guys," Justin said.

"Do you mind if I use your . . . you know." I

nodded toward the mini-bathroom. "The only other option would be the porta-potties, and given the choice . . ."

"Sure. See you out there."

Justin left the trailer, and I hit the head. When I came back out I noticed Frank holding a bright blue cell.

"You get a new phone?" I asked.

"Not mine," said Frank. "Justin forgot it."

Suddenly the door swung open, and Sydney popped her head in. "Justin," she began. She saw it was just us and frowned. "Oh."

"He just got called to the set," I explained.

"He left his cell." Frank held it up for her to see. "Should we bring it to him?"

"Please don't," said Sydney. "He shouldn't be getting calls while he's working. Just leave it here."

Frank laid the phone down on the counter. Sydney quickly stepped inside and shut the door behind her. "While I have you two alone, can I ask you something?"

"Sure," I said.

"You haven't known Justin for very long, but, well . . ." It seemed as if she was trying to find the right words. "Do you think he's been acting strangely?"

Frank and I looked at each other. Should we tell

her the truth or not? Then I decided—she cared about Justin and should know. "Yes, actually," I said. "It started in Atlantic City, once Ryan left."

"I thought so too!" she exclaimed. "So it isn't just me." She sat on a chair and leaned forward. "Now I want you to tell me the truth. It won't get Justin in trouble, I promise. Is there any reason I should worry about his behavior? More than usual, that is."

"What do you mean?" Frank asked.

She bit her lip. "In his world, and at his age . . . well, you always worry about bad influences. Drugs. Drinking. That kind of thing."

"We've never seen any evidence of that," said Frank.

"Really," I assured her. "Nothing at all."

She looked relieved. "That's great! Do you think you could kind of keep an eye out for that sort of trouble? I'd rather deal with it myself than have it come out because of a DUI or a story in a tabloid."

"Absolutely," I said.

"You got it," Frank added.

"Now let's go take care of our boy!" she said.

"It's going really well," Rick Ortiz told us. They'd been shooting an hour and were ready to change the camera positions, so everyone got to take a break. I watched Emily go back to her trailer, but Justin jumped up onto a loading dock and pulled out his cell. He made a couple of calls, and then started texting.

What is wrong with that picture? Then I remembered. "Hey, did you give Justin his phone?" I asked Frank.

Frank looked at me like I was a little on the dim side. "Uh, you were there? Sydney asked me not to."

"Check him out." I nodded toward Justin, who was chatting away. Then he flipped the blue device shut and slipped it into his pocket.

"He's Justin Carraway," Frank reminded me. "He could have lots of phones. One for every day of the week. One with streaming video, one with—"

"Okay, okay, you're right," I said.

Rick walked up to Justin and handed him a plate of food.

"Or," my brother continued, "someone else could have brought it to him. People are constantly running errands for him."

"Must be nice," I murmured. Yes. I admit it. Sometimes I envied Justin. I mean, how could you not?

But I wouldn't want the whole Justin Carraway package. The fans could get totally psycho, people tried to sponge off you, and you were always surrounded. It must be hard to know who your real friends were.

That made me want to find Ryan even more. Justin might deny it, but he really needed his twin. Ever since Ryan vamoosed, Justin had been a lot more on edge.

And that made everyone around him nervous.

Hong Kong Challenge

I was watching TV in my room after the shoot that night when my phone rang. "The timing is perfect!" Sydney Lamb gushed.

I held the phone away from my ear. She was speaking very loudly. Probably because of all the noise I could hear in the background.

"The timing of what?" I asked.

"The premiere of *Hong Kong Challange*, of course!" Sydney said. "The film needs to shoot the flying scenes over the next few days, and now that Justin isn't going to do them I can set up some other appearances. Isn't that great?"

"Yeah, sure." I couldn't figure out why she was telling me this. I already knew about the shots—

Rick had shown us the shooting schedule earlier.

"It's all been arranged," Sydney went on. "You and your brother have tickets to the premiere and the party at Glow, the new hot spot. And the hotel held more rooms than we actually need, so we've got space for you! Happy, darling?"

"That's awesome, Sydney!" I exclaimed.

While we were in Atlantic City, Justin had invited us to attend the premiere in New York City, but he hadn't mentioned it again. I had wondered if we were still going. He seemed to be running hot and cold toward us these days.

"What's awesome?" Joe asked, coming into my room.

I gestured for him to be quiet, then snapped my fingers, hoping he'd understand that I wanted something to write with. He just stared at me.

So much for brother-to-brother telepathy.

Sydney was blabbing a mile a minute, and I darted to my desk. I wrote the details on the back of an envelope. "Yup, got it," I said.

"And you know that request I made about keeping an eye on . . . things?" Sydney said. "It goes double in New York."

Now I understood. Even if Justin hadn't invited us, Sydney was going to make sure we went to New York City to help babysit. That was cool with me.

I actually liked the guy and didn't want to see him going down a bad road.

And if I had to attend a major movie premiere in the Big Apple, well, who was I to argue?

I clicked off with Sydney and grinned at Joe.

"So?" he said. "You going to tell me what that was all about?"

"What's it worth to you?"

Joe lunged at me, but I held the envelope out of his reach.

"Glad I didn't unpack," I said, "'cause I've got a party to go to in New York City!"

Joe managed to snatch the envelope out of my hand. "The premiere?" he asked.

"Yup. They've given Justin a couple of days off, so we can hang up there for a few days."

"This is turning out to be a really great summer vacation!" said Joe.

"Five-star all the way," I agreed. "I don't think we're even going to have to work to convince Mom that we should go."

"Aunt Trudy is going to be so jealous," Joe said.

"I wonder if the director is annoyed," I said. "Justin has these days off because they're shooting the flying scenes."

"The ones Justin swore he'd be able to do," Joe said. "I don't get it. How did he get such great reports from his flying teachers in L.A. and then totally freak during a simple descent on our way to Atlantic City?"

I shrugged. "I'm just glad we managed to land in one piece." I flipped open my phone again. "Speaking of one piece . . ."

I dialed Tom Huang in Atlantic City. Before Phillip Yu went into the ocean, the crime lord had been trying to recruit Tom to join one of his gangs. Hopefully, now that Phillip was gone the syndicate would leave him alone.

"So far so good," Tom said after I asked him. "And while you're in New York, there are some great restaurants you should check out in Chinatown."

"Are they the kind of restaurants where you're not sure you want to know what you're eating?"

"Exactly!" Tom laughed. "My mouth's already watering. Maybe I'll come join you."

As I hung up, Dad walked into the room. "Thought you'd want to know. William Bost has been sentenced and is being transferred to prison today."

Bost was the president of the Cleen Teens organization—and Justin's stalker. We were able to stop him before he took out Justin by switching prop bullets for real ones. "Glad to hear it," said Joe.

"He still insists he had nothing to do with the murder of the paparazzo, though," Dad added. "So it really might be an unrelated crime."

"Maybe Elijah took a picture that someone didn't want published," Joe suggested.

Dad nodded thoughtfully. "His camera was never found. The murderer could have taken it."

"Elijah was mostly tailing Justin," I pointed out.

"That guy was tailing anyone and everyone," Joe argued. "We were just so focused on Justin's stalker that we didn't think about anything but a link to Justin."

"Links to Justin. Right," Dad continued. "We're still investigating his manager's involvement in the bootlegging scheme."

"I hate to think that Slick was the industry insider," I said. "We really believed he was doing everything he could to protect Justin and Ryan in the business."

"Money makes people do crazy things," Joe said. "We've seen that time and time again."

"So far nothing has turned up in Slick's bank accounts to indicate he was involved in something on the side," said Dad. "Untangling the illegitimate bootleg business from Phillip Wu's legit businesses will take awhile. But don't worry—ATAC agents are on it. We'll keep you informed."

▲ Joe

"Yeee-ahh!" I burst through the swinging doors of the movie theater with a hard kick. We had just watched the premiere of *Hong Kong Challenge*, Justin's newest movie release. It had me totally psyched.

I whirled around and crouched in a defensive pose. I slowly moved my hands into position for a hard chop. "Time to kick it up a notch," I growled at Frank, quoting the movie's soon-to-be-famous catchphrase.

Frank just raised an eyebrow. "Really?" he said. "Here? Now?"

I glanced around. Paparazzi lined two sides of the red carpet (yes, it really is red). Anything I did would wind up on the net, on some gossip show, or in a tabloid. "You got a point." I straightened back up. "Where's Justin? He wasn't sitting anywhere near us."

"Probably meeting and greeting other famous people inside," Frank speculated.

"Or preparing himself for the onslaught," I said, eyeing all the reporters and star watchers.

"There must be a million cameras and reporters here," said Frank.

People stood along the edge of the carpet, holding mikes and speaking into film cameras. Sydney

Lamb paced along the sidelines. She was probably worried how Justin would behave. Sometimes he really played to the press. Other times . . . well, there was a reason he was a favorite of the tabloids. He could put on quite a show. Sometimes he was the hero and sometimes he was the villain. Which was it going to be today? Flip a coin.

We stepped out of the way of the stream of celebs now exiting the movie theater. The cameras started clicking, people started shouting, reporters raced up and down the carpet trying to get to the stars. It would be easy to get trampled.

I spotted Justin's blond head coming through he door. "There he is!" My eyes widened. There was another, shorter blonde next to him.

Emily Slater was arm in arm with Justin Carraway. Nothing unusual about two movie stars attending a premiere together.

Except these two teen movie stars hated each other. Emily even told me that she wished Justin was dead for all the grief he had given her. She was so serious that she had made it to our suspect list when we were looking for Justin's stalker.

"Do you see what I see?" Frank exclaimed.

"The truce of the century?" I asked. We watched as Emily and Justin slowly made their way along the carpet, smiling and posing for the cameras. At one point Emily even stood on her tiptoes to give Justin a kiss on the cheek.

Sydney came over to join us. "Is the Emily-Justin romance back on?" I asked. "Or is it an act for the press to promote the next film?"

"As far as I can tell, it's real," Sydney said, an amused look on her face. "Go figure."

We waited by the limo that was supposed to take us all to the party at the nightclub Glow. Emily and Justin stopped in front of us, turned, waved at the reporters, and slid into the limo. We climbed in after them.

"So what did you think of the movie?" Justin asked, draping his arm across the backseat behind Emily.

"Totally rocked!" I said truthfully.

"Gonna be a megahit," said Frank.

"Ryan's martial arts lessons really paid off," Justin admitted.

"I'm surprised they didn't just ask your twin to shoot those scenes," Emily teased. "It would have saved the director a lot of time having to do reshoots! Ryan's the black belt, after all."

I tensed. Would Justin get mad?

"I should have suggested that myself," Justin said. "I would have had a lot more time to hang out by the swimming pool."

"That's definitely more your style," said Emily with a grin.

The limo pulled up to the club for the party. There were even more onlookers, reporters, and cameras here. This time Emily and Justin just waved and strode quickly through the velvet ropes held aside by the bouncers. Justin paused long enough to indicate that we were part of his group, then vanished into the club. Once we made it past the ropes, the bouncer put them back to keep out the crowd.

A wave of music blasted us as we stepped inside. Colored lights flashed in sync to the thumping bass. Gyrating people crowded the sunken dance floor. Booths and balconies circled the huge space. Justin started bouncing to the beat.

A red-haired woman wearing a miniscule black dress stood behind a podium. Sydney stepped up to her and said something I couldn't hear over the music. The redhead scanned a guest list, nodded, then pointed. Sydney gestured for us to follow her. We snaked our way through the packed club to a booth. As Frank and I slid into the cushy seat, Justin grabbed Emily's hand and pulled her toward the dance floor.

Sydney whipped out her PDA and stared texting. Frank grinned at me. I knew I wore the same wicked grin. I'd seen stuff like this in movies and on entertainment TV shows—and here we were, right in the middle of it. Frank and Joe Hardy—A-list partygoers, surrounded by celebrities.

"Schmooze time." Sydney slid out of the booth. "Keep an eye on our boy!" She vanished into the crowd.

I watched a cute girl with short, dark curls laughing with a bunch of equally cute girls. "Isn't she the mean one from the reality show *It's All Mine*?"

"Never saw it," said Frank. "I like my reality real."

Justin and Emily reappeared at the table, holding hands. He was grinning ear to ear, and I'd never seen Emily this happy before.

"I need something cool to drink," Justin announced. He turned to Emily. "How about you?"

"Club soda with lemon *and* lime," she answered.

Justin looked at me and Frank. I was halfway out of my seat, figuring he was expecting us to go and get the drinks, when he said, "Anyone else?"

"Uh, a cola?" Frank said, sounding just as surprised as I was that Justin was going to do his own fetching.

"Me too," I said, sitting back down.

"Two colas and a club soda with lemon *and* lime," Justin said, bowing to Emily. "Coming right up."

"I'll help you carry," offered Frank, getting up.

I watched their progress through the crowded room. This was the hottest, trendiest, fanciest club in hot, trendy, fancy New York, so most of the people here were as famous or rich as Justin. So he didn't get the same kind of notice that he did when he went out in Bayport. Still, a lot of the girls were trying to get his attention. But Justin completely ignored them. He seemed to have eyes only for Emily.

Emily beamed, never taking her eyes off him either.

"So what gives?" I asked. "The dillweed turned into a bouquet of roses?"

Emily giggled. "I did kind of hate him, didn't I?"

"More than kind of," I said.

"Right after he came back from Atlantic City, he apologized for every stupid thing he had done," Emily explained, her eyes getting all dreamy. "He said after being away in Atlantic City, and after Slick was murdered, he finally came to his senses. Got perspective."

"Hmm." I watched Justin and Frank navigating the crowds on their way back to the table. I hoped this change wasn't just another temporary flight of fancy for Justin. He had already broken Emily's heart once. It would be pretty ugly if he did it again.

"Atlantic City was good for you," I said to Justin as he sat down.

"What?" Justin asked. "Why would you say that?"

He sounded offended, as if I was insinuating something.

"Going there turned out to be good for you and Emily, anyway," I explained, wondering what his problem was.

"Oh, oh, yeah," he said. He smiled at Emily. "Really good for *us*." He took her hand and squeezed it.

Sydney danced up to the table fifteen minutes later. "Sorry to be such an adult," she shouted over the music, "but we should think about calling it a night."

Justin and Emily looked disappointed.

"Justin, you have that interview tomorrow," Sydney reminded him. "Need to get your beauty sleep!"

Justin shrugged. "Okay."

Wow. No argument? No figuring out a way to get around Sydney? I guess Justin really *had* turned over a new leaf.

Justin led Emily through the mobs of dancers. Frank and I trailed behind them.

"Hey, wait a second," I said. "*I* don't have an

interview tomorrow. I don't need *my* beauty sleep."

"Have you looked in the mirror, dude?" Frank taunted. "You've missed far too much already. It ain't a pretty sight."

I punched his arm, but followed him out of the club.

The moment Justin and Emily stepped outside, the paparazzi jumped into action. Cameras clicked, people shouted questions, and flashes went off everywhere.

Justin held up Emily's hand and smiled at the crowd. "You can all be the first to know that Emily and I are back together. And this time I'll make it right."

Emily blushed twenty shades of red and smiled like she'd won the lottery.

"Will you and Emily do more films together?" someone yelled.

"Is there a sequel to *Hong Kong Challenge* in the works?"

"How do you feel about Slick being murdered?"

At that last question Justin froze, and all the color drained out of his face.

I was just as stunned. How could anyone ask a question like that?

But that one awful question unleashed a torrent of others. The reporters were like sharks who smelled blood in the water.

"Do the police have any leads?"

"Who's going to be your manager now?"

A short, stocky reporter pushed his way to the front of the crowd and shoved a microphone right under Justin's nose. "Do you feel responsible for Slick's death?"

Justin stared at the man as if he couldn't believe what he was hearing. I know *I* didn't believe it.

"What about the tabloid reporter?" the guy continued. "Elijah Gorman. Do you feel responsible for that murder too?"

Before anyone could react, Justin lashed out. He grabbed the guy's mike and whacked him across the face with it.

FRANK

4

Red Carpet Rumble

I stood there like everyone else, mouth open, eyes wide. It was as if none of us in the crowd could process what had just happened.

But in a nanosecond—total mayhem.

The reporter Justin hit let out a bellow. He dropped his camera and reached for his nose. I saw blood oozing out between his fingers.

The crowd of reporters and photographers surged in toward Justin. Some took snaps of the injured reporter, others clicked and yelled questions at Justin.

Justin flung his arms over his face and stumbled backward into Emily. She shrieked and toppled over in her high heels.

Now the photographers shoved and pushed one another to get a picture of Emily sprawled on the sidewalk in her fancy dress.

"Out of my shot!" someone shouted.

"Quit blocking me!"

Time to break this up. If they started fighting, I had a feeling it would be Justin who would be blamed.

"Going in!" I shouted at Joe.

"Right behind you!" he hollered back.

I shouldered into the group and grabbed a raised arm. No clue who it belonged to, I just didn't like the fist. I tugged it, and the reporter whirled and slammed me with his free hand. My head whipped around, and I saw stars. But I didn't let go.

Over the brawl I heard Emily screaming, Sydney shouting, and Justin cursing. I hoped none of *that* would wind up as an endless loop on the Internet.

"You going to behave?" I growled into the guy's ear. I had his arm twisted behind his back.

"Let me go, you stupid kid!" he shouted. "I'm trying to get my shot."

"You're taking shots, all right," I said, "but not with your camera. And I don't like it."

I glanced behind me and saw Joe duck a punch and grab a scrawny guy by his camera strap. They tussled, and Joe dragged the guy farther away from Justin.

Finally the cops arrived. I wondered who called them; I know I never had the chance. The crowd immediately broke up. I'd never seen a swarm of mostly pudgy, middle-aged guys vanish so quickly.

Justin and Emily stood near the entrance to the nightclub, both looking miserable. The paparazzi guy who had started the whole thing leaned against a car, holding his head back, with a tissue shoved up his nose.

"Justin, take Emily inside," Sydney ordered. "Get some sodas, cool off, have some fun. Let me handle this."

Justin nodded. He put his arm around Emily and guided her back into the club.

"I want to press charges!" said the paparazzo.

"No, I don't think you do," Sydney snarled. She was in full pit-bull mode. "We have witnesses who will be happy to identify you as the cause of this near riot!"

"Like me," said Joe, stepping forward.

"And me," I added, coming up beside him.

"So what's it going to be?" the police officer asked.

Sydney glared at the reporter. Joe crossed his arms and frowned. I gave him my meanest scowl.

"Forget it," the guy muttered.

The cop went back to his car and drove off.

Sydney faced off with the reporter. "How could you do that to a teenager?" she demanded, her hands on her hips. "He just lost someone very close to him. And you asked if he felt *responsible*? What's the matter with you?"

I'd never seen her like this. She was like a mama bear defending her cub. Which in a way she was.

"Back off, lady," the reporter whined. "I didn't mean anything by it. It just seems like bad luck is following Justin these days. This fight proves my point!"

"You were just trying to get a rise out of a vulnerable kid to sell your stupid papers," Sydney snapped.

"All I'm saying is, knowing Justin Carraway is a dangerous thing. Just ask my nose and my equipment!"

I couldn't actually argue with him on that. It did seem as if Justin always attracted trouble—or found himself in the middle of it.

The reporter shook his head and shambled away.

"I would have smacked him myself," said Sydney, shaking her head. "Too bad Justin beat me to it." She pulled out her ever-present cell and started texting as she strode back into the club.

Now that the cops were gone, paparazzi were slowly showing up again. There was also a growing crowd of people trying to get into the club.

"So what do you think?" I asked. "Should we go back inside?"

Joe grimaced. "I don't really feel like being the third wheel."

"Good point," I said. "If Justin and Emily get any more lovesick, I think I'm going to *get* sick."

"Sydney has got Justin in her sights," Joe pointed out. "I think we can go off babysitting duty now."

"We just have to make it through the crowd," I said. "Man, people go out seriously late in this town!"

I scanned the people surrounding the entrance, looking for an easy escape route. Then I saw some faces that were far too familiar.

Three large, muscular Asian men in very fancy suits.

I couldn't believe my eyes. Joe and I had tangled with these powerhouses just a few days ago. They worked for the crime lord Phillip Yu. His bodyguards.

I knew all too well how good they were at their jobs—they were expert martial artists. Joe and I helped keep Tom Huang from getting his butt totally kicked when they went after him on Phillip Yu's orders.

That was back in Atlantic City.

So what were they doing here? Now?

Dead Man Walking?

As soon as Frank elbowed me in the side, I saw exactly what had him so freaked. Phillip Yu's goons.

SUSPECT PROFILE

Name(s): No idea. But there are three of them.

Hometowns: Various cities in China

Physical description: Lean, mean, killing machines.

Occupation: Bodyguards to international businessman and crime lord Phillip Yu. Currently out of work due to the sudden demise of their boss. Or so we thought.

"No way!" I blurted. "What are they doing here?"

One of the men caught my eye. His jaw tightened, and he said something to the two men with him.

"We've been spotted," I told Frank. "And they know we know they know."

Frank gave me a confused look. "Uh, I think I understood that."

The three men spun around and faded into the crowd.

"I want to know what they're up to," I said.

"Right behind you, bro," said Frank.

We sprinted after them. They hurried around a

corner, and we picked up speed. We didn't want to lose them.

My heart nearly jumped out of my chest as a car screeched to a sudden stop just inches from me. Squealing tires and honking horns shrieked around us as we darted between yellow taxis. As I rounded the next corner, I saw the three goons vanish into a limo. Frank dashed up beside me.

"They're in that car," I told him.

"You mean the one headed straight for us?" asked Frank. "Jump!"

We flung ourselves out of the street. I stumbled and went sprawling on the sidewalk. Frank reached down and pulled me up—hard.

"Hey! I need that limb!" I complained, yanking my arm out of his grip.

"Check out the backseat."

I peered at the car speeding away from us. "There's another person in there with them," I observed.

"Does that look like who I think it looks like?" Frank asked.

"Can't be," I said. "Can it?" I squinted, trying to see into the tinted back window. I turned to Frank. "That's *not* Phillip Yu, is it?"

Frank looked as puzzled as I felt. "His body was never recovered," he said slowly.

"Could he have somehow faked his own death so he'd be able to get away?" I wondered.

"I guess anything is possible," said Frank. I could hear the doubt in his voice. I don't think either of us really thought Phillip Yu was still alive. But you never know. I've been surprised by some pretty wacko turns of events as a member of ATAC. What was one more?

"There's a more important question," Frank went on. "What were they doing at the premiere party?"

"I can top that," I said. "What we really want to know is, who were they there to see? Justin? Or us?"

"Good point." Frank nodded. "Phillip acted like there was bad blood between him and Justin, so Justin could be the target. But he dropped out of that helicopter because of us."

"So you're thinking this could be payback time?"

"I have no idea," Frank admitted.

We walked back to the club. There were still loads of reporters around—it was a club favored by high-profile people—but it was a lot calmer. I had an idea. "I want to take a look at tonight's premiere party guest list."

"What do you think you'll find?" asked Frank.

I shrugged. "Maybe it's all just one big coincidence.

Maybe Phillip's guys were here trying to spot celebrities like all these other people."

Frank raised an eyebrow.

"I know, lame idea, but I'm still going to check it out."

Frank and I went back into the club. I strolled up to the red-haired hostess and flashed her my best Joe Hardy smile. Hey—it works, I swear. No matter what Frank says.

"I was wondering," I said to her, "is there a Phillip Yu on the list? He's been bugging me about getting in, and I just want to make sure it's cool."

The girl looked at her clipboard. "No problem. He's on it."

I gaped at her. "He is?"

She looked puzzled. "I thought you wanted him to get in," she said.

"Oh yeah, yeah. I just . . . never mind."

Frank and I quickly melted into the crowd. "Why would he be on the list?"

"Someone put him on it," said Frank. "I bet Sydney will know who."

Sydney was rocking back and forth in time to the music while texting. When she noticed us approaching, she waved us over and gave us each a quick hug. "Thank you so much for your help out there earlier," she said. "I hope you weren't hurt."

"We're fine," I assured her.

"Good. I'm trying to get that idiot fired."

"Listen, we were wondering about the guest list," I said.

"Too late to add any of your friends now," Sydney scolded. "That list was compiled more than a month ago!"

Now I was even more confused.

So was Frank. "But you didn't know us a month ago, and we're on it," he said.

"Getting A-list people to attend requires advance planning," Sydney explained. "Don't be insulted, but the reason there was room to include you was because some of the people who had said yes ended up saying no."

"Got it," Frank said.

"So you decided who went on the list?" I asked.

"I did, but so did Slick. Justin too, of course. Even Ryan had input," said Sydney. "Oh, must run. There's Wendy Mellington. I've been wanting her to interview Justin forever. Time for a little ego stroking!" Sydney wiggled her way through the dance floor and gave air kisses to a woman with the biggest earrings I'd ever seen.

"Phillip must have been invited back when Justin was still into the high-stakes poker games out in Vegas," Frank reasoned. "At some point they were pals."

"So the bad blood between them is a recent phenomenon," I said. "Wow, I just thought of something weird. Sydney was able to include us because of Phillip's drop into the ocean."

"So we're here in his place," said Frank as we headed toward the door. "You're right. Kinda freaky."

"Maybe his bodyguards were on the list too," I realized.

"It would be useful to know their actual names," Frank said. "Let's check."

We approached the hostess at the podium again. "Why did you walk away so fast?" she asked. "You rushed off before I could tell you not to worry about a thing."

"What do you mean?" I asked.

"Your friend Phillip didn't have any trouble getting in," she said. "He arrived long before you asked about him."

Mind freeze. Was I hearing what I thought I was hearing?

"Phillip Yu," I said. "He—he was here?"

"Yes." She looked down at her list. "But he came alone. He didn't bring his date. He may have already left. I only check them as they come in."

"Th-thanks," I stammered.

"Can you describe him?" Frank asked. "We just

want to be sure we're talking about the same guy."

"Sure," said the hostess. "An Asian guy wearing a very expensive leather jacket."

I looked at Frank. "Yeah . . . ," I said, feeling more and more like I was in the twilight zone. "That sounds like him."

"Can you tell us anything else?" Frank pressed. I knew he didn't like the idea that Phillip had been here any more than I did—for so many reasons.

"Sorry," the hostess said. "I didn't pay that much attention. You can't keep VIPs waiting. I hurry everyone through as quickly as possible." She smiled. "I hope your friend had fun."

"I'm sure he did," I said. Nearly running us over in a car. That was *exactly* Phillip Yu's idea of fun.

This was one strange turn of events.

"Good luck finding him," the hostess called after us as we headed for the door.

We stood on the sidewalk outside the club. Neither of us moved. I think we were just too wigged out.

"Well," Frank said finally, "there's one thing we know for sure. Phillip's muscle knows we saw them."

"So who does that put in danger?" I asked. "Justin—or us?"

Yo, Ho, Ho

"**C**heck out those tall ships," I said.

"Check out those soccer players," Joe countered.

We were down near the very bottom of Manhattan, at the South Street Seaport, for Justin's photo shoot. Justin would be playing a marine in an upcoming movie, so the magazine thought it would be fun to do the pictures on board one of the ships.

South Street Seaport is really cool. It's kind of a mall, but the streets and the buildings all look like they're from colonial days. The piers have a bunch of restored boats to tour, but there are all kinds of other events too. Today there was a stage set up with some guys demonstrating slick soccer moves.

I wasn't exactly sure what that had to do with seafaring days, but it looked fun.

"This place is packed!" Emily commented.

"Luckily, it's so crowded no one will notice us," said Justin. "I want to be the only one paying attention to you."

Emily giggled. "And I'd better be the only one you're paying attention to!"

"You're thinking of the old Justin," Justin said. "I'm the new and improved model."

"So true!" Emily beamed and slipped her arm around him.

"You're not so improved if you keep the journalist waiting," I reminded Justin. "We have to get through this crowd and to the end of that pier."

"We'd better hurry, then," Justin said. "I don't want to have to walk the plank."

We hurried across the street, past the double-decker tourist bus and around the carts selling souvenirs. Big signs were set up announcing tours and a pirate re-enactment on one of the ships. As we rounded the tables set up for a model boat-building contest, I got a great view of the ships. They were real beauties.

"Avast, me hearties," said Justin. "I believe our destination is in sight."

"Arrrrrrgh," Joe growled in pirate agreement.

Up ahead at the end of the pier was a group that had to be the magazine people. There was a woman surrounded by photography equipment talking to a college-aged guy. They were with a bald man wearing what looked like a tool belt—only instead of hammers and wrenches, it held hair and makeup brushes. A woman dressed a lot like Sydney—super trendy—paced nearby. When she spotted Justin, she waved.

"The reporter is Jessica Winters," Emily whispered as we approached the group. "She interviewed me when I was cast in your movie. She's really nice."

"Good to know," Justin said.

"Hello, Justin," said Jessica. "Emily, nice to see you again. This is our photographer, Caroline Jeffers, and her assistant, Mark Cranshaw. And Rocko is our hair and makeup genius."

Everyone nodded at everyone else.

"And you are?" Jessica asked me.

"I'm Frank Hardy, and this is my brother, Joe." I tipped my head in his direction. "We're PAs on the film, and Justin invited us along for the premiere."

"So we're all hanging together in NYC," Joe added.

"What happened to your old entourage?" Jessica asked Justin. "A falling-out?"

Justin laughed. "No, nothing like that. They're just all back in L.A."

Good save. She obviously had wanted a little dirt, but Justin wasn't going for it.

"I see the rumors are true," Jessica said. "You and Emily are an item?"

"More than an item," Justin replied. "We're soul mates."

Emily blushed and leaned into Justin. "Absolutely."

"Let's get set up for the shots, and while Caroline does that, I'll ask some questions."

"Sounds like a plan," said Justin. "Where do you want me?"

We all traipsed after Jessica onto a schooner, which, according to the sign, was built in 1895. "We rented it for the interview," Jessica explained. Several guys in matching Seaport T-shirts hung around the deck. I figured they were there to be sure nothing happened to us—or to the restored ship—while we were aboard.

It was a nice-size ship, but compared to the behemoth moored right in front of it, the schooner looked like a toy.

Caroline and Mark started doing light readings

and fiddling with the umbrellas pros use to control the lighting.

"Why don't we start with how things are going with you two," said Jessica, turning on a teeny-tiny recorder.

"Great," Justin said. "At least *I* think so. What do *you* think?" he asked Emily. I could tell by his huge smile that he already knew her answer.

"Better than great," Emily confirmed.

"I'm sure all the girls out there want to know what it's like to be Justin Carraway's girlfriend," said Jessica.

"Well, he's so sweet, and really generous." Emily held up her pendant for Jessica to see. "He gave me this today. Every morning I find a new present waiting for me!"

I was impressed. He really was trying to make up for being such a jerk to her in the past.

"And how do you spend your free time?" Jessica continued. "I imagine with the film shoot you don't have much."

"Not since Justin got back from Atlantic City," Emily admitted. "But before . . ."

Jessica looked expectantly at Justin. "Before . . . ," she prompted. "What kinds of things did you do?"

Justin looked blank for a minute. "Uh . . . uh . . . let's see. There was that restaurant . . . ?"

Uh-oh. Looked like Justin's past behavior as a total hound was catching up to him.

"You remember, honey-boo," Emily prodded. "We went horseback riding. And our favorite hang-out was that burger joint, Topper."

"Oh, right!" said Justin. "How could I forget?"

"Honey-boo," Jessica repeated. I wondered if she was trying not to gag. I know I was. "That's a cute little name. Justin, do you have a special pet name for Emily?"

Again the blank stare. I had a feeling Justin was going to have to get Emily an even better present tomorrow to make up for this today.

Emily gaped at Justin. I could see she was starting to get peeved. "Justin!" She pouted. "I can't believe you forgot what you used to call me!"

Justin took both of her hands in his. "That's the past," he said, his voice soft. "I only want to think about the future."

"Oh, Justin." Emily sighed. She turned to Jessica. "You see? Isn't he the most delicious?"

This was getting way past sickening. Joe had strolled away—he must have already had enough of the sugar overload.

I joined him at the side of the ship. "Good spot to be if you need to hurl," I said.

"No joke." Joe laughed, then glanced over at Emily

and Justin again. "I've seen Justin as Mr. Charm, Spoiled Brat, and King Flirt. I've never seen him like this."

I shrugged. "I guess that's what *luuuuuuuuuv* can do to a guy."

Joe clapped both his hands on my shoulders. "Promise me if I ever get like that you'll give me a nice hard kick."

"Deal," I said.

Joe and I explored the schooner as Jessica continued her interview and Caroline took photos. It was really cool. I liked the old-fashioned look of it. I could see why the magazine thought it would be a good spot to shoot Justin's interview. It really had a pirate feel. Even though the seaport pier was insanely crowded, I felt nicely apart from everyone by being aboard the schooner.

"Yo, ho, ho, ye landlubber," Joe said to me. "Looks like they're taking a break."

"We should let Justin know that Phillip's bodyguards were at the premiere," I said. "Just in case they're after him, we want him to keep his guard up."

"Good idea. And we should break the freaky news that someone's using Phillip's name—"

"Or Phillip himself," I put in.

"Or Phillip himself was at the club."

"But we should tell him alone," I said. "Do you think we'll be able to tear him away from Emily?"

"They have turned into Siamese twins," said Joe. "I have an idea. Follow me."

I walked across the slightly rolling deck. The ship was moored, but the wake of the other boats in the river created nice little waves.

Joe went up to Jessica. "Hey, maybe you should take some pix of the happy couple," he suggested. "And some of just Emily."

Emily immediately perked up. I knew she wanted the whole world—and by that I mean her potential rivals—to see that she and Justin were in love.

"I'd be happy to," Emily said.

"I guess it wouldn't hurt," said Jessica. "Caroline, you cool with that?"

Caroline shrugged. "Whatever. Hon, you should check your makeup, though." She turned to the bald guy. "Rocko?"

"I'm on it," he said.

I smiled at Joe. Between primping and taking pictures, Emily would be busy and we could talk to Justin.

"Hey, Justin," I said. "Can we talk to you a minute?"

"Sure." He pulled a soda from the cooler the ship guys had provided.

"Up here." We walked up to the bow of the boat and looked out over the water.

"There's something you should know," I started.

"Just a heads-up," Joe added. "Not because it's dire or anything."

"Ooo-kay," said Justin, frowning. "What's up?"

"We saw Phillip Yu's bodyguards at the premiere," I told him. "And someone using Phillip Yu's name was at the party."

Justin's face went totally white. "What are you talking about?" he shouted. "You told me Phillip was dead. What is wrong with you? You can't even get one simple fact straight!"

I took a step backward. Justin's fury surprised me. I was totally unprepared for it.

"I'm in danger, aren't I?" Justin demanded. "Jeez! That guy tried to run me over with his boat! Or don't you remember that?"

Joe looked as confused as I felt. *We* always thought Phillip was dangerous, but the whole time we were in Atlantic City, Justin completely downplayed the idea that Phillip might mean trouble for him. He behaved as if they barely knew each other. Now he was acting as if he was deathly afraid of the guy.

"What are you saying to him?" Emily suddenly appeared at Justin's side. "Why are you stressing out my honey-boo?"

"It's nothing," I said. "Just some news that took Justin by surprise."

"Yeah, well, if you two—" Justin cut himself off. Either he didn't want Emily to know the details, or he just didn't want to get any more upset.

"Break's over!" Caroline called. "Ready for some new shots!"

Justin took a deep breath. Emily stroked his arm. "Just forget all about whatever these guys said to you," she cooed. "Everything's all right."

Justin took in another breath, then smiled. "All better. Because of you," he said to Emily.

"You two should leave," Emily ordered. "We can't have anyone upsetting Justin during the interview."

Justin glared at us. He obviously felt the same way.

"Fine," I said. "No harm meant."

Justin and Emily returned to the mast, where Caroline had set up more lights. As they started posing, we headed for the gangplank. Joe grabbed my arm.

"Are those Phillip's guys?" He nodded up toward the large historic ship moored just in front of our schooner.

I shaded my eyes. There were three dark-haired men in suits standing at the stern of the ship. They seemed to be watching the shoot. "It's too far away for me to see. I can't even tell if they're Asian from this distance."

"Let's get closer."

We raced down the gangplank. We darted through the tourists and dashed up onto the deck of the enormous ship.

"Do you see them?" I asked.

"They're heading the other way," Joe said.

"Come on!"

We started toward the bow—then we heard the explosions!

Hit the Deck!

My first thought was for Justin and Emily. Did Phillip's guys do something? Sabotage the ship? Shoot a weapon with major firepower?

"I can't see anything!" Frank shouted. "Too many people!"

He was right. There was a crush of tourists all around us. I had to see if Justin was all right—and find out if the three men we had spotted were actually Phillip's goons.

But how?

Then I saw a solution.

I grabbed the rigging that led up to the top of the enormous sail. I started climbing. Frank saw what

I was doing and clambered up the rigging on the other side.

The strong wind made it tough to keep the rope ladder steady. I managed to twist around to get a look into the little schooner far below me.

Justin and Emily lay on the deck. Caroline was clutching her equipment, and her assistant Mark was trying to keep the light stands from toppling over onto the deck, which was rocking violently from a pronounced wake. Jessica and Rocko were leaning over the side of the boat, trying to figure out what was going on.

"I see the three guys!" yelled Frank. "But they're already leaving the pier."

"Justin's okay," I called back. "What caused the explosion?"

Frank twisted around to get a view of the other side of the ship. "Uh, false alarm," he called.

"What?" I demanded. "What are you seeing?"

"Off to starboard," Frank said. "Another ship."

"Another ship was firing at us?" I said. "That's crazy!"

I had to see what he was talking about, but my position on the rigging had me facing the wrong way. I slipped my foot off the rope rung and snaked it around the outside of the rigging. I replaced it pointing the opposite way. It was an extremely awkward position, and I quickly reached around and grabbed the rope. I was able to shift my whole body around, though I set the rigging swinging. I gripped the ropes hard and concentrated on steadying myself.

Instantly I saw that Frank was right. A new ship had appeared starboard—that was what had created the powerful wake. It was full of people in pirate costumes, and there was a smoking cannon in the middle of the deck.

I had the really unpleasant feeling that we had just made major fools of ourselves. That's when I remembered the poster advertising some kind of reenactments. I guessed we were in the middle of one of them.

"You! Get down from there!" a furious voice below us shouted.

"Uh-oh," I said. "Do they put people in jail for unauthorized climbing?"

"I don't know," said Frank. "But I have a feeling we aren't going to be welcome to come back any time soon."

We quickly descended the ropes. By now there were three guys wearing Seaport T-shirts surrounding us.

"You can't climb the rigging!" the bearded one yelled at us.

I had to come up with something quick. No way were we going to go to jail, pay a fine, or walk the plank. "You've done a great job," I told the group. Frank stared at me like I was crazy, but I just went on. "We can absolutely recommend this location. Your security is top-notch."

"What?" the bearded guy snarled.

"Justin Carraway is over there being interviewed." I pointed toward the ship Justin was on. He was helping Emily to her feet. "He was thinking about having a private party here." I started walking away, hoping Frank would follow. "We can honestly report that it's an excellent idea. Very good job, sirs."

By now we were practically jogging. But they weren't stopping us. Frank and I waved, turned, and ran down the gangplank.

"That was a close one!" said Frank. "How do you come up with excuses like that?"

"Just my natural brilliance, I guess," I said.

We hurried back to the little schooner. Justin and Emily were still on the deck. Both looked pretty shaken. Justin probably would have handled the fake cannon fire better if we hadn't just told him about Phillip.

"It's all fine," I said. "Nothing to worry about."

Justin glared at us.

"I think the interview is over," Emily announced. Caroline and Jessica looked surprised. When did she become the boss? "Justin is too upset to continue."

He did look freaked. I guess hearing that a guy has risen from the dead can do that. And then thinking that he was being fired on by pretend pirates had to send a dude over the edge.

"I think we have enough," said Jessica. "Caroline?"

The photographer nodded. "Got plenty to choose from."

"We'll contact you if we need anything else," Jessica said.

As Caroline and Mark packed up the equipment, Justin and Emily left the ship and vanished in among the tourists.

"Where do you think they're going?" Frank asked.

I shrugged. "To buy Emily another present? Get some free ice cream samples?" I rubbed my stomach. "I could go for some of that too. I saw someone giving away mango-flavored ice cream."

"You can get ice cream later," Frank said. "We need to talk to ATAC. Try to find out if there's any chance Phillip survived his drop into the ocean."

I sighed. "I guess you're right. And that's not a

call we can make from tourist central. I guess it's back to the hotel."

A limo had driven us to South Street Seaport, but Emily and Justin must have taken it. So we had to find our way back to the hotel using the New York City subway system. That took awhile. The way Frank acted, you'd think I got us lost on purpose.

"Finally," he announced, flopping down on his bed. We were sharing a double room. "I thought I'd never see this place again!"

"Hey," I complained. "We weren't *that* lost."

I was about to hit the remote and see what was on cable when I heard a strange sound, like birds chirping.

"What's that?" I asked Frank.

"No idea." He looked puzzled. We started searching the room.

"It's in your overnight bag," I said.

"It's not mine," Frank insisted. He opened his bag and rummaged through his clothes. A knowing look crossed his face. He pulled out a slick-looking PDA.

"Phillip's," he declared. "It fell out of his pocket during our fight on the helicopter. I completely forgot I had it!"

"Answer it," I said. "It might be helpful to know who's trying to reach him."

Frank hit a button. "Hello?" he said. He paused. "No, who's *this*?" He looked at me and hit another button. "He hung up."

"Did you recognize the voice?" I asked.

Frank shook his head. "He sounded surprised that I wasn't Phillip." He looked back down at the phone. "I was about to hand this over to the cops when Rick showed up with the news about Ryan. I figured it would have evidence about the bootlegging ring."

"Everything got so crazy after that," I said.

"I never really unpacked after we got home from Atlantic City because we left again so quickly."

I raised an eyebrow. "Does that mean you're still wearing the same clothes? Do I need to stand downwind?"

Frank just rolled his eyes. He does that a lot. I wonder if I should be offended.

Then the PDA made a little beep. "Incoming message," said Frank. He held out the device so I could read the text with him.

Give it back. Or else.

I stared at the PDA and then at Frank. "Did we just receive a message from a dead guy?"

Texts from Beyond?

I stared at Phillip Wu's PDA. "Who sent this text?" I wondered.

"Whoever called you, I mean Phillip, on that thing now knows that Phillip doesn't have the PDA anymore," Joe pointed out.

"But why would the caller care?" I asked.

Joe shrugged. "Only way to know that is to find out who the caller is. See if the caller sent the text."

I scrolled through the log of incoming calls. No names appeared, so I wrote down the numbers. "We'll have to do some kind of reverse look-up," I said. I knew ATAC would have those resources.

"I want to know what's on the PDA that would make someone threaten us," said Joe.

I clicked buttons and found the document files. I opened one. "It's in Chinese," I said. I opened the rest of them. "*All* of them are in Chinese."

"We know someone who can help us with that," Joe pointed out. "Tom Huang. And he might have some inside info that even ATAC doesn't have. He knew a lot about Phillip's underground activities."

"Good idea." I quickly grabbed my own phone to dial Tom. I didn't want to add any numbers to the PDA's call log. At some point we were going to have to turn it over to the authorities, and I didn't want anything strange to turn up on it that

---

SUSPECT PROFILE

Name: Phillip Yu

Hometown: Hong Kong

Physical description: 6", late twenties, slim, longish dark hair, Chinese-American, supercool dresser; megarich and shows it.

Background: Murky. Lots of very successful legit business practices, but also leader of a dangerous Chinese gang operating in Hong Kong and Atlantic City. Maybe New York, too? High-stakes gambler.

Suspicious behavior: Lurking around the premiere with his goons?

Suspected of: NOT BEING DEAD.

would lead to complicated questions. Like why we were using evidence to make calls.

"Hey, Tom," I said when he answered. "Think you can come up to New York?"

"Love to," he said. "When?"

"Uh, how about now? We have something we need your help with, and I can't really go into it over the phone."

"Very mysterious. Sure, I can be there in a few hours. But I have one condition."

"Name it," I said, hoping he wasn't going to ask for something too hard to provide, like a role in Justin's movie or something.

"We have to go to my favorite restaurant, the Sleeping Dragon on Mott Street, in Chinatown. Why don't you meet me on Canal Street, and I'll take you there?"

"I think we can manage that," I said. "So, see you around seven?"

"See you then."

We spent the rest of the afternoon acting like typical tourists, checking out the Empire State Building, Central Park, that kind of thing. Then we headed back to the hotel.

"We still have some time," Joe said. "Want to hit the pool?"

"Sure," I replied.

We changed into our suits—lucky thing Joe looked up the hotel's amenities before we packed—and went up to the rooftop pool.

The pool area was empty except for a lone guy lying on a lounge chair. I recognized that blond hair even from the back. Justin.

I was about to call out hello, when I noticed something. On the little table beside him was a glass of what looked like water—and a small pill bottle. I grabbed Joe's arm so he'd hold back. Just as I feared, Justin took a small white pill out of the little bottle and then washed it down with a swig of water. Then he stashed the bottle in a gym bag.

Was Sydney right? Was Justin on drugs? That might explain some of his erratic behavior. I glanced at Joe and could see he was wondering the same thing.

Justin stood and stretched, then turned around. He looked startled to see us. I wondered if he was worried that we had seen him take the pill. If he was, he covered it quickly.

"Hey, guys," he greeted us with a big smile. "That was pretty crazy down at the seaport."

"Sure was," I said.

"Yeah, I can't believe we thought that re-enactment was real!" Justin said, laughing. He seemed to be in a much better mood.

"Where's Emily?" I asked.

"Shopping," said Justin. "I'm crazy about the girl, but really, there's only so many stores I can take in an afternoon."

"I hear you," I said.

"We're going to dinner later," Justin said. "Uh . . . you want to come?"

I laughed. "Don't worry, we won't crowd you. We're meeting a pal from Atlantic City in Chinatown."

"He's making us go to this restaurant, the Sleeping Dragon, on Mott Street," Joe said. He shuddered. "I have a feeling he's going to try to gross us out with the strangest food he can find."

I gave Joe a light punch on the shoulder. "Don't be such a wimp."

"I'm not a wimp," Joe protested. "But my stomach is."

Justin had to run to meet Emily, and we waited until we saw him step into the elevator. "We have to find out what kind of pills those were," I said.

"Man," said Joe. "I was really hoping Sydney was wrong."

"Me too, bro," I said. "Me too."

"It's like a different city," I commented as we climbed up the subway steps and got our first look at Canal Street. We were at the edge of Chinatown.

The street was completely packed with people. What made it even more crowded were all the tables set up on the edge of the sidewalks. They were mostly covered in exotic fruit—some I'd never even seen before.

Opposite the street were shops, but they looked more like booths since they didn't seem to have doors. They sold everything you could imagine: jewelry, DVDs, souvenirs, shoes, and more. Items hung from the ceilings and the walls and were piled up on boxes in front.

All the street signs were in both English and Chinese. I noticed that some of the stores had signs only in Chinese characters. Most of the people around were Chinese.

"There's Tom," Joe said, waving.

Tom loped toward us with a big grin on his face. "Hello, Hardys!"

Tom was a cool guy. He was kind of a tour guide for Chinese customers taking the buses from Chinatown in New York to Atlantic City. He told them stories, brought them to different casinos, and helped arrange other activities. But what he was really into was movies, and he was thrilled when we got him a job working on Justin's film when we were on location in Atlantic City.

He was also super grateful when we saved him from Phillip's goons. We weren't the only ones who thought his Atlantic City connections would be useful—Phillip Yu had been pressuring Tom into joining his syndicate.

"How's the movie going?" Tom asked.

"Great," Joe told him. "How's the tour guide gig?"

"Not as much fun as the film," Tom admitted. "But it keeps money in my wallet. Come on, let's go to the best restaurant in Chinatown."

The sidewalks were so packed we had to walk in single file. We followed Tom through narrow, twisting streets. With the sun starting to set, it was pretty dim; we were not in a very well-lit area. I looked up at a cool-looking pagoda-style building with a curving roof and bright red pillars and did a double take—it was a Starbucks!

We stopped to allow a guy carting big tubs of fish packed in ice to pass. My nose wrinkled—it was pretty smelly around here. I turned my head to get a less direct hit of the stench and thought I noticed someone quickly duck into a doorway.

We continued walking. I had been trying to keep track of where we were going, but the streets curved around so much I no longer had any idea. Then the back of my neck prickled. Not good.

That usually happens when I'm being watched or followed. I snuck a look over my shoulder, but I didn't see anyone. I glanced up ahead at Joe, wondering if he had the same feeling, but he had already crossed the street, so I couldn't ask him.

Tom finally stopped. "This is it!" he announced with a big grin.

"Are you sure you didn't take us all the way to China?" Joe joked. "That was some hike."

This little hole-in-the-wall was the best restaurant in Chinatown? It didn't even have a sign out front. Good thing Tom brought us here. We'd never have been able to find this place ourselves.

I peered through the grimy window. "Looks like all the tables are full," I said. I figured the fact that the place was packed was a good sign.

"Of course!" said Tom. "Best noodles in all of Chinatown. Dumplings, too."

As we stepped through the door, little chimes rang. A tiny middle-aged Asian woman scurried out of the back, wiping her hands on her apron. When she saw Tom she beamed.

"Tommy!" she exclaimed. She and Tom chatted enthusiastically in Chinese. She smiled broadly at us, then led us to a table near the back counter, where the cash register was and several people were waiting for take-out orders.

"For you," she said, gesturing to the table. She vanished into the back.

We sat down. "She forgot to give us menus," I said. "Should I go grab some?"

"No, no," Tom said. "She'll just bring us what she thinks we should eat."

I hoped her idea of good was the same as mine. I guess Joe wasn't the only one with a wimpy stomach.

I heard the little chimes, and then a customer strode up to the counter. My mouth dropped open.

It was Mr. Wong, a dealer at a very high-stakes table in Atlantic City.

"Hi, Mr. Wong," Tom called.

Mr. Wong turned. When he saw me and Joe, he looked equally surprised.

"What brings you here?" he asked, coming over to our table.

"Tom," Joe replied. "He claims this is the best restaurant in Chinatown."

"He's right," said Mr. Wong. "Mae, the owner, is my cousin."

"Small world," I said.

"Especially in Chinatown," Mr. Wong said. "Many people are related in this neighborhood."

"Remember, I told you that Atlantic City is a popular destination for people living in Chinatown," Tom said.

"Some of us relocated," Mr. Wong added. "But our ties to Chinatown are very strong."

I felt a vibration in my back pocket, then heard the sound of birds. Phillip Yu's handheld was ringing. I pulled it out and quickly shut it off.

Mr. Wong stared at the PDA and then at me.

Uh-oh. He had probably heard that very distinctive ringtone often. Phillip Yu had been a regular player at Mr. Wong's table. He was going to wonder what I was doing with it.

"Have you heard about Phillip Yu?" Mr. Wong asked.

That kind of came out of nowhere—or did it? Was he trying to figure out if this really was Phillip's phone? Or maybe the question was totally innocent. He hadn't seen us since Philip fell out of the helicopter, and hearing the ringtone may have simply reminded him of Phillip.

"Phillip Yu?" I repeated. "No, nothing." I turned to Joe. "You?"

Joe shrugged. "Did he win big or something?"

I was glad this was one of the times he picked up on my lead.

Tom's eyes flicked from me to Joe. He obviously couldn't figure out why we were lying. But he was confused enough not to contradict us.

"Tragic," said Mr. Wong. "He had some sort of helicopter accident. Drowned."

"That's awful," I said.

Mae came out of the kitchen with a bag.

"Ah, my dinner," Mr. Wong said, taking the bag from Mae. "Well, good to see you again."

"I don't get it," said Tom after Mr. Wong left. "Why did you play dumb about Phillip?"

I tapped the PDA. "Because of this."

"It's Phillip's," Joe explained. "And we want to know why someone wants it back so badly they'd threaten us for it."

JOE

9

Chinatown Showdown

Tom stared at the PDA. "How did you get Phillip's device?" he asked.

"It fell out of his pocket when we were up in the helicopter," I said.

"I picked it up and then forgot about it until we got here," Frank added.

"Who knows you have it?" Tom asked.

"Whoever called and sent this text." Frank picked up the PDA, scrolled through the menu, and found the text message. He showed it to Tom.

"Whoa," he said. "They sound serious. What do you think is in there?"

"Evidence of the bootlegging ring," said Frank.

"And who knows what else," I added. "But Phillip

81

was tidy. He must have cleared his logs on a daily basis."

"We searched through the files," Frank told Tom. "But they're in Chinese. We were hoping you'd be able to translate."

Tom fiddled with the buttons and screens on the PDA. "Can you print them out for me?" he asked. "I'm not totally fluent, and I'll need to read slowly and carefully. There's a lot here. It will be much easier as hard copy."

"Sure thing," Frank said. "We'll get it downloaded and overnight it to you."

"This is definitely a rush job," I said. "Someone really wants this back, and we want to know why. There are probably all sorts of files important to the case."

"Got it."

Mae came to the table with a bowl of steaming noodles. They smelled great. We dug in. I'm happy to report there wasn't a single scary dish.

After stuffing ourselves, we walked Tom to his bus stop. Now that the sidewalk peddlers were gone, the streets were really deserted. Some areas were pretty dark, and most of the stores were closed.

The express bus that went direct between China-town and Atlantic City was under an elevated subway bridge. The arches supporting it were massive, and every time a train passed the sound was deafening. There were ten or twelve other people—all Chinese—waiting for the bus too.

We didn't have a long wait. A bus lumbered around a corner, letting out a wheeze as its brakes engaged and the door opened.

"Well, this is me," said Tom. "Are you going to be able to find your way back to the subway?"

"Sure," I said, though I actually wasn't all that confident. "We just need to find Canal Street and we're golden."

Tom boarded the bus after promising again to make the translation a priority. We waved as it pulled out. Then Frank and I were left under the dark bridge alone.

"So, which way?" Frank asked me. "You seemed to know the way back."

"Uh, well, I knew that we had to find Canal Street. Now, where that is, I can't exactly tell you."

Frank rolled his eyes. Again. I really had to call him out on that later.

"I say we should just head toward any street that looks like a major thoroughfare or is well-lit. It's bound to get us to Canal Street," I went on, hoping I sounded confident.

"We'll also try to find a store that's open and ask directions," said Frank.

"If that makes you feel better," I said.

"I think we passed one of the streets we took when we walked to the restaurant from the subway. So let's head thataway."

We began walking, and I thought over all the strange events of the last weeks. "This is one freaky case."

"That's because we don't even know what the case is," Frank said. "All we know is that a lot of weird things have been happening."

"We need to get a handle on what's going on."

"It seems like we've got two things going on. Something with Phillip and the PDA—"

"Probably related to the film bootlegging business," I pointed out.

"And we've got Justin running hot and cold," said Frank.

"Which may be a result of doing drugs," I said. "And we have Ryan somewhere out there and impossible to find."

"Let's start with Justin," Frank suggested. "We'll maker a list and see if that gets us anywhere."

JUSTIN'S STRANGE BEHAVIOR

• Acted like he didn't know Phillip; Phillip acted like he knew Justin.

• Isn't worried about Phillip; is scared to death of Phillip.

• Suddenly responsible during shooting; skipping parties to learn his lines.

• Madly in love with Emily; couldn't stand her last week.

• Madly in love with Emily but can't remember things they used to do together.

• Very nervous, very jumpy, sometimes likes us, sometimes doesn't.

• A LOT less laid-back.

• Doesn't seem worried about his own twin's disappearance, even though everyone else is.

"Does this add up to drugs to you?" I asked.

"Could be. But you know what I see from this list? Justin only started to get weird once Ryan disappeared."

"Yeah," I said, nodding. "Remember in Atlantic City when the director said his performance was off? That it just wasn't the same as the scenes they'd shot before? Slick asked Justin if it was because Ryan wasn't around."

"Ryan's a lot more important to Justin than even *he* realizes."

"And to the Justin fame machine."

"Phillip is on this list," Frank commented. "Could

what's going on with Justin have anything to do with Phillip?"

"I don't see how, but who knows?"

PHILLIP

• Phillip jumps out of the helicopter but may have been at Justin's premiere.

• Phillip seemed to have it in for Justin in Atlantic City.

• Phillip was on the guest list—they were friends at some point.

• Phillip's bodyguards—are they tailing us or tailing Justin?

• Someone called Phillip's PDA. Did he know Phillip was dead or not?

• Someone wants this PDA back—is it the same person?

• Who murdered Slick and why? How does it relate to the fact that he was the industry insider?

• Does ANY of this relate to the murder of Elijah Gorman?

I threw up my hands. "I say let's make everyone a suspect. Suspected of: complete strangeness."

"Once the files are translated, we'll have a lot more answers," said Frank.

The birds chirped again. Frank pulled the PDA

out of his pocket. "Another text," he said.

He held it out to show me.

> This device doesn't belong to you. Leave it at the
> foot of the Confucius statue in Confucius Square.
> Now. Or suffer the consequences.

"I don't even know where we are now!" I protested. "How are we supposed to find that statue?"

Frank wore a grim expression. "We have a bigger problem," he said. "Whoever sent this message knows we're in Chinatown."

"You're right." I dropped my voice. "Do you think we're being watched right now?"

"Wouldn't be surprised." Frank made a fist and banged it into his thigh in frustration. "I thought we were being followed when we were on our way to the restaurant."

I gaped at him. "Why didn't you say anything?"

Frank looked sheepish. "I should have. But I wasn't sure, and I didn't want to freak out Tom."

"We need to get someplace better populated," I said. "Pronto."

We picked up our pace. A few blocks up ahead there seemed to be more light—and more street traffic.

When things are dicey, I sometimes get what

feels like 360-degree vision—a heightened sense of everything around me. And that sense was telling me we were being followed.

"Someone's behind us," I whispered to Frank.

"Let's face the threat head-on," Frank whispered back. "There are two of us. I'm only hearing one set of footsteps."

We whirled around, ready for anything.

Okay, maybe not anything.

We weren't prepared for the dude standing in front of us dressed all in black, with a ski mask totally covering his face.

The ninja attire on a hot summer night wasn't the problem.

It was the little silver gun pointing straight at us.

Race Across Rooftops

For one second I actually thought it was a joke. First of all, the outfit was straight out of some cheesy movie. But it was the gun that made it hard to take seriously. It just didn't look real. It was small, silver, and seemed to have some kind of ornate decoration on it.

Another second later my brain kicked in—and so did the fear.

"Give me the PDA," the masked man said.

His voice was low and growly, as if he were trying to disguise it. He was about the same height as me, which meant it could be one of Phillip's bodyguards. The black garb was loose so it was hard to tell if he was built like the powerhouses I'd seen in action before.

I didn't want to wait to find out.

Screeech! The sound of a speeding taxi rounding the corner startled the gunman. In the split second he looked over his shoulder I shouted, "Run!"

Joe and I booked it out of there. *If we can get to an area where there are people, we'll be safe,* I told myself. *He's not going to open fire surrounded by witnesses.*

The thudding footsteps behind me told me he might catch up to us long before we got to a major avenue.

"Divert!" Joe shouted to me.

He pulled ahead and rounded a corner. I followed him, hoping we could lose the gunman. I spotted a fire escape ladder. "Up!" I yelled to Joe. If the guy chasing us saw which street we'd run down, he might not notice us if we were above him.

I jumped and grabbed the metal rung, then pulled myself up and planted my feet on the ladder. I scrambled onto the fire escape, then quickly raced up to the next level, Joe right behind me. I took a moment to breathe, then started up to the next landing, hoping we'd lost the guy.

Pow! Pow! The sound of gunfire and the whiz of a bullet zipping by my head told me otherwise.

I covered my head with my arms and kept going up. We made it to the roof.

"Are we cool?" Joe asked, panting.

He heard the footsteps clattering up the metal fire escape the same moment I did.

"No—we're still piping hot!" I cried. "We need another way down!"

Joe raced to the door that led into the building, while I charged across the roof to see if there was another fire escape on the other side.

Joe dashed up beside me. "It's locked."

I stared into the alley below us. "And there's no way down."

"We've got to do something," said Joe. "We're sitting ducks up here."

"No kidding."

I studied the building across the way. In this part of town the buildings were narrow and crammed together. "I think we've got to jump."

"You serious?"

I glanced behind me, just in time to see the hood of the ski mask start to rise above the edge of the roof. "Serious as a heart attack."

I backed up, even though I knew that brought me toward the gunman and my goal was to be as far away from him and his gun as possible. But I needed the running start if I was going to make it across the gap between the buildings.

Joe darted beside me. "One, two, three . . ."

"*Go!*" I pumped my arms and legs as hard as I could, picking up speed as I approached the edge of the building. Never slowing for a moment, I bent my knees to give myself the strongest launch possible.

I was airborne.

A moment later I landed hard and went sprawling on the roof next door.

Made it!

I heard Joe land beside me. I say I heard him because, yes, I shut my eyes when I made the leap.

"Is he still following us?" Joe asked.

I pushed myself up and immediately slammed back down. The dude was firing again!

"Doesn't this guy ever quit?" Joe said.

"Let's not stick around to find out." I rolled away, wanting to get to the other side of the roof. There had to be a fire escape we could use to get down.

I hadn't made much progress when I realized that the shooting had stopped. And Joe and I were still on the roof alone. Could he have finally given up—or run out of bullets?

"What do you think?" asked Joe.

"Don't know."

Joe carefully and slowly raised himself inch by inch to check out the other rooftop. Then he straightened all the way up. "All clear," he said.

Something shiny caught my eye. I crept over to it and realized it was a bullet. "I wish I had a plastic bag with me."

"What did you find?" asked Joe, dropping down beside me.

"Evidence," I said. I fished around in my pocket and pulled out a gum wrapper. "This will have to do." I picked up the still warm bullet in the shiny foil. "Don't want my fingerprints on this baby."

I pulled out the PDA so I could slip the bullet in below it in my pocket.

"Oh, man," Joe groaned. "Do you think it will still work?"

"Huh?" Then I looked at the PDA.

I stared at the shattered screen and the banged-up casing. "I must have crushed it when I landed on the roof," I said.

I looked at Joe. "Did I destroy our most important piece of evidence?"

Desperately Seeking Data

Frank looked so bummed that I didn't have the heart to tell him that I thought the PDA was toast. "We might still be able to pull off the files," I told him.

"I hope so," Frank said. "Let's get this baby to the tech doctor quick. I don't want anything else to happen to it."

We climbed down the fire escape and discovered that our run through Chinatown and up and over buildings had brought us right to Canal Street. The hotel was our first stop—after rolling around on the roof, we looked pretty much the worse for wear. And we needed to research places that would still be open, where we could download files and ship them out overnight. That required a phone book or internet access. All back at the hotel.

The elevator opened onto our floor, and we discovered Emily pacing back and forth outside the door to Justin's room.

"Hey, what's up?" I asked. "Waiting for Justin?"

Emily opened her mouth, but before she could speak there was a crash from Justin's room. "That is totally unacceptable!" he shouted.

"Who's he fighting with?" asked Frank.

"His accountant," Emily said.

"At this time of night?" I asked. It was already after ten p.m.

"He's in California," Emily explained. "Three hours earlier. Besides, Justin said it was an emergency."

Another crash came from Justin's room. "You work for *me*!" Justin yelled. "I can have you fired!"

"What's the problem?" I asked.

"Justin wants some more money, but the accountant won't release it."

"Why would he have to ask his accountant for it?" asked Frank.

"The money he makes is in a trust," Emily explained. "That's how it is with most actors who start as kids. We're given an allowance, but everything else we can't touch—usually until we're twenty-one." She frowned. "It can be really annoying. I mean, it's *our* money! *We* earned it. But someone else decides how much we get and when."

"That would annoy me, too," I said.

"But Justin always seems flush," Frank said.

Emily shrugged. "He's short right now. In fact, he canceled our dinner plans and—" She glanced around to be sure no one would overhear her. "I think it's because he didn't have enough money. But you can't let him know I told you. He'd be so humiliated!"

"We won't," Frank promised.

"We know how it is for a guy to feel like he can't take his girl out," I said. "Been there myself." Though Justin's allowance was a *lot* heftier than mine.

"Does Justin fight with the accountant a lot?" asked Frank. "I'd hate it if I had to ask permission all the time."

Emily shook her head. "As far as I know, this is the first time they ever had a fight about it."

I tucked that piece of info away. He was certainly spending a lot more these days because of all those daily gifts to Emily, but could there be something else requiring cash? According to Rick, Justin used to get into high-stakes games out in Las Vegas, and that costs money. But he wasn't into that scene at all in Atlantic City.

A dark thought entered—but one I couldn't push aside. Drugs cost money. This could be more evidence that Sydney's fears were all too well-founded.

"I hope that all works out," Frank said, nodding toward Justin's door. "We should get out of here before Justin comes out."

"Good idea," agreed Emily. "He'd hate it if he knew you heard this."

We went to our room and changed out of our roof-rashed clothes. "That guy must just blow through money."

"Why is it so bad now?" Frank wondered.

"Hey remember his memorabilia website?" I said.

"Justin Time?" said Frank. "What about it?"

"Maybe he's always been a lavish spender, and the way he made up the difference was with the sales through the website. That way he'd have cash he wouldn't have to ask the accountant for."

"Could be. Maybe sales have been down or something, so he hasn't had the usual supplement."

"You check in with Vijay," I said. "I'll find us a place to download the PDA."

By the time I had located a place that would print out files and another place that would messenger late-night mail, Frank had gotten some info from Vijay.

"Sales on the website have been kind of low for a while," Frank informed me. "But there was just a bump—probably thanks to the premiere."

"So that's not a big moneymaker," I concluded.

"Not big enough for Justin's current needs, anyway," Frank confirmed.

A new thought occurred to me. "Maybe the Phillip thing and the Justin weirdness are linked," I said.

"In what way?" asked Frank.

"At some point, Phillip and Justin were on good enough terms that Phillip was invited to the premiere party," I said, ticking off points on my fingers. "Rick told us Justin had been into high-stakes gambling in Vegas. Justin avoided Phillip in Atlantic City." I turned and faced Frank. "What if Justin owes Phillip money? The goons are here to collect, and Justin is freaking out."

Frank nodded. "I think you're onto something, bro."

I grinned. "See—beauty *and* brains. I'm the total package."

"Please don't make me have to hurt you," Frank said. "That still doesn't explain who's after the PDA, but at least it helps make sense of some of what's been going on."

The twenty-four-hour computer place I'd found, the Geek Squad (their term, not mine!), was just a few blocks away. There were a few people surfing the Net at the bank of computers up near the window. Two bored-looking clerks chatted behind a counter.

Frank and I strolled up to the counter. One of the clerks was a girl with a pierced nose; the other was a guy with two-toned hair.

"How can we help you?" the girl asked. Her voice was really sweet, despite her tough exterior.

"We're hoping you can salvage some data," said Frank. He pulled the PDA from his pocket.

The girl raised an eyebrow—which made me notice that it was also pierced. "You and the device have a difference of opinion?"

"Long story," I said. "Is there any hope for the patient?"

The girl looked skeptical. "I'll see what I can do."

"We need to have all the files downloaded as hard copies," Frank explained.

The girl nodded. "Give me about half an hour." She took the PDA and vanished into the back.

We killed time by checking out all the techno-toys. Eventually the pierced girl came back with a stack of papers.

"Looks like it worked!" I said.

"There were a lot of files on here," she said. "But here you go." She handed me the papers.

"This is great," Frank said with a total look of relief. I knew he had been worried that he'd destroyed critical evidence. "Can we copy them here?"

"Sure." She nodded toward the row of copiers. Frank paid for her work, and I started the copying.

"Ready?" Frank asked, joining me at the copier.

"We now have two sets ready to send off for translation, and one to hang on to," I said.

We went to a twenty-four-hour place that could deliver the files to Tom and to ATAC the following day. We slipped the bullet Frank had snagged from the roof into the envelope going to ATAC.

Before we sealed it, Frank looked at the PDA. "Do you think we should send this to ATAC too?" he asked.

I narrowed my eyes, thinking. "I know we should," I said slowly. "It *is* evidence. But . . ."

Frank nodded. "I know. If we get more calls or texts, it might help us understand what's going on."

"Let's keep it for now," I suggested. "They're getting the files."

We sealed up both envelopes and handed them over to the clerk for delivery.

"Calls!" Frank exclaimed as we left the shop.

"Huh?"

"If that girl was able to download the files, I bet the PDA still has the numbers in the call log."

"From our mysterious caller and text sender," I said.

"Yup," Frank declared, looking at the PDA. "Still here!"

I fished out my phone and punched in Vijay's number. "Vijay is going to be sick of hearing from us."

The call went straight to voice mail. Unlike New York City, Vijay wasn't a 24-7 guy.

I left him the numbers and told him we needed reverse look-ups and that ATAC would be receiving important evidence tomorrow. I also let him know we'd be back in Bayport then too.

"I think that's it for now," said Frank.

"As long as we're not chased by three martial artists or a guy all in black with a little silver gun, I'd say we can call it a night."

We arrived home the next afternoon and reported to the set. They were still shooting scenes down by the docks in Bayport. We had just parked our motorcycles when Justin stepped out of his trailer. His back was to us, but we could see him pop something into his mouth and then take a swig from his water bottle.

"Drugs?" I whispered to Frank.

"I think we need to find out."

We hung back until Justin rounded the corner. We "casually" leaned against his trailer as two crew guys carried cables past us. Then we yanked open the trailer door and snuck inside.

"We better be quick," Frank said. "No idea how long Justin will be gone."

"I hear you."

We began rummaging through Justin's stuff. I felt kind of creepy—I wouldn't want anyone going through my room. I have to admit, my room is a lot messier than Justin's trailer. It would be a lot harder to find anything in there. I'll remind Frank of that next time he gets on my case about what a slob I am. It's all part of the camouflage plan, I'll tell him.

"Got it!" said Frank. He held up a small vial. "Nothing written on the label, though."

"So that means he didn't get them from a doctor," I pointed out. "Looks bad."

"For all we know, they're just headache pills and Justin just likes to keep them in these containers," Frank reasoned. I could tell, though, that he didn't believe that any more than I did.

"Well, once ATAC analyzes them we'll know for sure."

"Let's get out of here before Justin comes back,"

Frank said. He dropped one of the pills into the small plastic bag he had brought with him and shoved it into his pocket.

He cracked open the door. "Coast is clear." He slipped out, and I followed him quickly. No one had seen us.

"Where does Rick want us?" I asked. Our cover was that we were *working* on this film, not sneaking around checking up on the star. We needed to actually do our job.

"He said to go down to the docks and keep stray people from walking through the background."

"Got it."

We passed the area where the scene was going to shoot. Justin and Emily were both getting final touch-ups to their hair and makeup, and the director and the assistant were checking the monitor and discussing camera angles. Rick looked like he was doing ten things at once. He was basically a blur.

We edged around all the cables and equipment. They weren't actually shooting on the docks, but I could see that if anyone walked by they'd wind up in the shot. Our job was to stand around and make sure no one did that.

Easy gig. The docks were basically deserted. No one would have any reason to walk through.

"If we stand here, we shouldn't be visible," Frank

said, stationing himself at the edge of an abandoned warehouse.

I scanned the area. "Yeah, if anyone is going to be coming by, it would be from that direction." My brow furrowed. "Like right now. Is that . . . Belinda Conrad?"

Frank blinked a few times. "Uh, yeah, I think so. What's she doing here?"

"Think she's going to make another play for Justin?" I asked.

When Justin was shooting in Bayport before, he and Belinda went out—very briefly. She had gone kind of gaga for him, but when he flirted with other girls in front of her and basically dissed her, it crushed her.

This was all complicated by the fact that she usually crushes (in the other sense of the word) on Frank. Why? Haven't a clue. Unlike her jerkoid brother, Brian, Belinda is sweet, cute, and a catch.

Only Frank couldn't seem to decide whether or not he wanted to be caught. He acted like a complete idiot around her. But he acts like that around most girls.

"This should be interesting," I said with a grin.

What can I say? Watching my brother turn beet red and stammer is amusing to me. Don't judge me. You'd find it funny too.

"Hi, guys," Belinda greeted us.

"Belinda," said Frank. Well, "mumbled" is more accurate.

"So, you're still working on the movie?" Belinda asked.

"Yup."

My brother. What a conversationalist. I had to help him out.

"So what are you doing down here?" I asked. "Come to check out the shooting? Maybe take a peek at Justin?"

Now it was Belinda who blushed.

"No, nothing like that," she said. "Actually"—she turned her big eyes on Frank—"that's kind of what I wanted to talk to you about."

"You want to talk to me about Justin?" Frank looked confused—and as if he wished he could be anywhere but standing in front of Belinda.

Then I saw something that made me wish the same thing.

Coming along the wharves, heading straight toward the pier, were three familiar suits.

Worn by Phillip Yu's muscle.

The Return of the Terrible Trio

I stared at my sneakers. It was a little easier to talk to Belinda if I wasn't looking at her. And if I kept my face down, maybe she wouldn't see I was blushing.

Man. It was as bad as an allergy—and just as involuntary. I had to get these reactions under control. For one thing, my discomfort was far too amusing to Joe.

"I'm afraid I acted, well, totally goofy around Justin," Belinda said.

"A lot of people do," I assured her.

"Frank," Joe said, "Belinda shouldn't be here."

"I don't think she'll show up in the shot," I said.

"Actually, I don't think we should be here either," Joe went on.

"What?" I picked my eyes up from the ground and planted them on Joe. "Rick assigned us to this spot."

"Then scan the perimeter," Joe instructed. "Just like we're supposed to do."

I couldn't believe it. Joe lecturing *me* on keeping my mind on my work? A pretty girl just had to cross into his radar and I'd have to struggle to get him to stay on point.

"I don't want to get you guys in trouble," said Belinda.

"Then scoot," Joe told her.

Now he was being downright rude. Was he jealous that she was paying attention to me and not to him? Because Joe is never rude to a girl. Well, almost never.

"Joe—," I started.

"I just want to talk to Frank for one minute," Belinda said. "And if you'd quit interrupting, I'd have finished by now."

"Fine!" Joe said, throwing up his hands. "You talk. And Frank, keep an eye out for trouble. And old friends."

Ding ding ding! Alarms sounded in my head and a lightbulb went on. Joe was trying to tell me something, and I had a feeling it wasn't good.

I scanned the area, and my eyes landed on three

all-too-familiar martial artists. Headed straight toward us.

"Joe's right," I said quickly. "This isn't really the best time to talk."

Now Belinda looked embarrassed and unhappy.

Joe must have felt badly for her. "Frank promises to call you later," he said. "Don't you, Frank?"

"Uh, yeah, sure. I'll call you later."

"I just wanted to say I hope you don't think badly of me," Belinda said. "Because I made such a fool of myself over Justin."

"You're being too hard on yourself," Joe told Belinda.

I probably should have said something too, but I was too busy gauging the speed of the bodyguards' approach.

"And he'll still call you later," Joe added. "Right, Frank?" He elbowed me in the side.

"You got it," I told her. "As long as you leave now."

She sighed. "All right." She started to turn, but I grabbed her arm.

"Not that way," I told her. "Go up through the set area." I didn't want her to cross paths with Phillip's men. I'd rather risk getting into trouble with Rick than make her a target.

"Just make sure you stay really close to the wall of

the building. You shouldn't be seen there," I added.

"Okay." She hurried away.

She was worried what I'd think of her because of how she acted around Justin. I wondered what she'd think of me because of this weird conversation.

But this wasn't the time to think about that.

"So what do we do?" Joe asked. "Run?"

"Too late for that," I said. "Besides, I want to find out what it is they're after."

The three guys strode up to us. Up close, they were even bigger than I'd remembered. They stood in a line, each with massive arms crossed over well-muscled chests.

One stepped forward. "You have something we want."

"A job on the movie?" asked Joe. "We can totally hook you up."

The guys didn't find that comment funny. One of them pulled aside his well-tailored jacket to reveal a gun. Not the little silver job the ninja-clone had used on us in Chinatown. This was a serious street weapon.

"No need to go there," I said. I fished the PDA out of my pocket. "I'm not even sure how to work the stupid thing."

I figured the less I seemed to know, the safer I was.

"So now are you going to leave us alone?" Joe demanded. "Justin, too."

"You got what you wanted," I added.

"It's all up to the boss," the guy who took the PDA answered.

"Who *is* the boss?" I asked. "Did Phillip survive that fall?"

The guys looked at one another, then burst out laughing. "Does that scare you?" one of them asked. Then they just turned around and walked away.

"Well, that was pretty useless," Joe commented. "We don't know any more now than we did before."

"We'll know plenty once ATAC and Tom go through the files," I said.

"It's a good thing we sent them off last night," Joe said.

My phone rang, and I checked the caller ID. I hit the button. "Hey, Tom, you done already?"

"Not even close," he said. I could tell from his voice he'd found out something. Something big. "I thought you'd want to know this right away. Justin was involved in the bootlegging scheme."

My jaw dropped. This was mind-blowing!

"Why would Justin be selling bootlegs of his own movies?" I asked. "That only diminishes his earnings."

Joe stared at me as I clicked off. "*Justin* was the

industry insider?" he asked incredulously. "Not Slick, like we all thought?"

"Looks that way."

"That makes no sense!" Joe was having as much trouble processing this as I was.

"It means he was working with Phillip Yu all along. Maybe the bad blood between them was because Justin wanted out. We saw for ourselves that Phillip doesn't like the word 'no.'"

"But when we got to Atlantic City, Justin acted as if he didn't even know Phillip," said Joe, still puzzling it out.

I shrugged. "Maybe he thought it would be a good cover? Keep their distance?"

Joe's phone rang. "Vijay," he announced. "Uh-huh. Uh-huh. You're kidding me! Thanks." He hung up, a stunned look on his face.

"Looks like the info you got is as weird as what I got from Tom."

"No kidding. How's this: The phone calls to Phillip's PDA came from Ryan Carraway's cell phone!"

"Okay, now this has gone over to the freaky side," I said. "Why would *Ryan* be contacting Phillip?"

"Vijay also said that the first text we got came from a disposable—no way to trace it."

"And the last one?" I asked.

Now Joe grinned. "That was sent by none other

than our friendly Atlantic City card dealer, Mr. Wong."

Finally, something I could understand. "He must have been working with Phillip all along. He's taken over for him, and now the terrible trio is working for him."

"That text came in right after he saw us with the PDA at the restaurant. The one telling us where to drop it off in Chinatown."

I frowned. "But that guy showed up with the weird gun right after that. He never gave us time to even get to the drop-off point."

"Probably didn't trust us to do it."

"I guess . . ." I smiled at Joe. "Well, one mystery is solved. We're not being chased by a dead guy at least."

Joe glanced toward the set. "Looks like they're taking a break," he said. "What do you think? Time to talk to Justin?"

"I hate to do it in the middle of a shoot, but I think we have to. We need to find out why Ryan was trying to reach Phillip—and warn Justin that he is about to be exposed for his role in the bootlegging ring."

We started walking back to the trailers. "I just don't get it," Joe said. "Why would Justin risk so much?"

"Could he have needed money that badly?" I

wondered. "He seems to have a cash flow problem right now."

Joe shook his head. "How can you blow through so much money?"

I tapped my pocket, where I had slipped the plastic bag with Justin's pill. "Makes drugs seem more possible."

"There's the gambling angle too, " Joe said. "Phillip's guys could be after him because he owed Phillip money. And maybe that's how Phillip got him to steal the films for him."

"This is all starting to fall into place," I said. "Though we still aren't sure if the terrible trio has been after Justin or us."

We knocked on Justin's trailer door. This wasn't a conversation I was looking forward to.

"Come on in," Justin called from inside.

We walked into the cramped space. "We need to talk to you. About something serious."

Joe leaned against the door. I wondered if that was because there weren't a whole lot of places to be in the trailer or if he wanted to be sure that Justin didn't make a run for it. "We know about the bootlegging scheme," he announced.

Justin looked startled, but then put his game face on. He was a high-stakes poker player *and* an actor, after all. "What about it?"

"Slick wasn't the industry insider," I said. "We know it was you. And very soon, so will the authorities."

He looked as if he was going to hurl. I guess going from everybody's favorite movie star to being a felon was a nauseating roller-coaster ride.

"It wasn't me!" Justin blurted.

"Sorry, buddy, that won't fly," said Joe. "It's all in the files on Phillip Yu's PDA."

"I swear it wasn't me!" Justin leaned his elbows on the table in front of him and held his head in his hands. "I can't believe I'm going to tell you this, but I guess I don't have a choice." He looked up at us and sighed. "It wasn't me. It was Ryan!"

"What?" I asked. Yet *another* twist in this totally convoluted case? My head was beginning to hurt.

Justin stood and paced. Well, he tried to. There just wasn't enough space, so he basically moved back and forth a few inches.

"That's why Ryan disappeared," Justin said. "I found out about what he was doing and told him to lie low. I promised I'd try to take care of it." He stopped moving. He looked miserable. "He's my brother. I had to protect him."

"He never did go to Isola, did he?" I said.

Justin shook his head. "I don't actually know where he went. We both figured that would be the safest way to handle this."

"But why would he do it?" Joe asked.

Justin shrugged. "I have no idea. Money? Revenge? Who knows?"

I nodded. I always thought it must be hard to be Ryan, living in Justin's shadow, watching him with the girls you like, getting all the attention, the tons of money. One day Ryan must have finally had enough and decided to do something to even the score.

Only he got in with a seriously dangerous crowd. And he was now going to face some serious charges.

Justin shook his head. "I'm just so worried about him. If he's exposed, I'm afraid he'll do something drastic. He's—he's a little unstable."

Whoa. The case just took an even darker turn. I wouldn't want to be responsible for Ryan trying to harm himself. But what choice did we have? We couldn't ignore this.

"Listen, do you think you can give me a moment?" Justin asked. "I need to get my head straight. They're going to be calling me to do another scene any minute."

"No problem," I said.

Joe and I left the trailer.

"You do realize he's probably alerting Ryan right now," said Joe.

"Yeah, I know. But Ryan has already disappeared. It's not like we know where he is now and can just go and get him."

"So we're back to trying to track down Ryan," Joe said.

"Only this time it isn't because he needs to be rescued from a hurricane," I added. "It's because he's a criminal."

Revenge of the Twin

A loud crash from inside the trailer made me jump. Then came another crash. This time it sounded like breaking glass.

"I have a feeling he's not alerting Ryan after all," Frank said.

"Interesting coping mechanism," I mused. "Smashing things. I need to try that."

"Not while I'm around," said Frank. "Wait— forget I said that. If I'm not around, it would probably be *my* stuff you'd smash."

Justin's tantrum ended, and the door to the trailer slammed open. I decided that now was not the time to suggest he tell Ryan to turn himself in. Let him cool down a little.

We watched Justin return to the set, and then we went back to our spot on the docks. This time there were a couple of kids hanging around skateboarding, but we were able to keep them from ruining any shots.

They worked for another hour or so, and then Frank said, "They look like they're wrapping up."

"Let's give Justin a chance to do the right thing. Get Ryan to turn himself in."

"I'm with you."

Frank and I jogged back toward Justin's trailer. As we did, we passed Emily. She did not look happy.

"What's wrong?" I asked her.

"Justin is being totally weird," she complained.

"I think he has a lot on his mind," Frank offered.

That was the understatement of the year.

"But we're in love! He should talk to me about what's on his mind!" Emily protested.

Frank and I exchanged a look. Justin's problems weren't exactly the type you want to share with a girl you just got back together with.

"Give him space," I suggested. "Then, when the time is right, I'm sure he'll talk to you."

Emily took a deep breath and nodded. "You're right. Thanks!" She spun around and headed for her own trailer.

We knocked on Justin's trailer again. "Hey, Justin,

it's Joe and Frank. We just want to talk a minute."

The door opened, but Justin didn't let us inside. "What's left to talk about?" he demanded. "You turn him in and Ryan's life is ruined. Why couldn't you just leave it all alone?"

"We don't want to hurt Ryan," Frank said. "But Slick was probably murdered over this bootlegging scheme. We don't want something like that happening to Ryan."

"Or to you," I added. "There are some heavy players in this operation."

Justin looked down at his feet. "I know. You're right."

"Do you think you can get in touch with Ryan?" asked Frank. "Talk him into turning himself in? Things would go a lot better for him that way."

"I—I just don't know." He shut the door.

"That went well," I muttered.

"Hey! Hardys!" Rick Ortiz called. "Can you help us load up?"

I stared at Justin's trailer door. There wasn't anything else we could do here. We might as well get back to our "real" job. "Sure."

"So I guess this means this location is done," I said to Joe as we headed for our motorcycles. Most of the crew had left already.

"Yeah, I think there's something in the park tomorrow, and then back to L.A. to finish up in the studio."

The sun had set while we were packing up the equipment. The actors had all disappeared long ago.

"It's still hard to wrap my mind around all this," I said. "Ryan was stealing from his own brother, but Justin covered it up."

"What's harder to get is motive," said Frank.

"Like Justin said—money?" I suggested. "That's often a motive."

Frank wasn't convinced. "Yeah, but Ryan never seemed to need money. It was Justin who spent like crazy and was just demanding money from the accountant. Ryan seemed pretty levelheaded about all that."

"Okay, then revenge? Jealousy? He had that big crush on Emily and got on Justin's case about how he treated her."

"That almost makes more sense than money," Frank mused. "Only it would be a secret kind of revenge: If Ryan hadn't been caught, Justin would never have known about it."

"Maybe that's how Ryan wanted it. Knowing he had something over Justin, and his super-twin had no clue."

"I guess that's possible."

I grinned at Frank. "So, you have any big secrets you're holding out on? Revenge for my great looks, winning personality, and ultimate charm?"

"You wish."

"Maybe this whole mess is why Justin started taking drugs," I said.

"Bad idea."

"You know that, and I know that, but . . ."

"I hear ya."

"I'll feel a lot better once we get the results from ATAC on the pills," I said.

"And the bullet. With our description of the unusual gun, maybe they'll be able to figure out the shooter."

"Let's hope. Though I'm pretty sure it will lead back to Phillip's goons."

"You mean Mr. Wong's," Frank corrected. "He's running the syndicate now."

"Not for long. Not after we bring him down."

We climbed aboard our motorcycles. I pulled on my helmet and revved the engine.

Have I mentioned how much I love my bike?

It was one of those perfect summer nights for a ride. The big full moon made it easy to see, and the breeze I kicked up offset the muggy weather.

Riding was a great way to clear my mind after all

the craziness of the case. Sometimes I do my best thinking on a long ride. And at this hour there was very little traffic to worry about.

I could hear Frank keeping pace with me, a few yards behind.

We left the industrial area and were cruising through the residential section. I wasn't that familiar with this part of town, but I was pretty sure we were coming up to the park. So far we'd made it on all green lights, but I saw that we were going to hit our first red.

I braked.

Only my bike didn't.

I twisted the grip with my right hand again. Nothing. I pushed down with my foot to try the back brakes. Still nothing.

My heart thudded hard as it hit me.

Someone had tampered with my brakes.

Sabotaged

I couldn't figure out why Joe wasn't slowing down as we approached the intersection. I don't think I've ever seen him run a light. Well, I wasn't going to do it, and I would definitely get on his case about it later.

My right hand twisted the brake control—and then I understood.

Something was wrong with my bike—Joe's, too.

I tried the front brakes and then the back. Nothing. No response.

This was bad. Really, really bad.

I was still able to accelerate, so after a quick glance in both directions I barreled through the intersection.

Who would sabotage our bikes? screamed in my brain. But I had to worry about that later. Every brain cell had to focus on controlling the bike and figuring out a way to end this insane ride without killing anyone—including myself.

I tried to remember the geography of this area. There was a park up ahead.

Because I'd accelerated, I was now riding next to Joe. "The park!" I shouted. "Try to pile into some bushes!"

"Find the sledding hill! Maybe it will slow us down!" Joe hollered back.

The park was up ahead. I prayed there wouldn't be any traffic between here and there. Luckily, we'd spent such a long time loading the vans, it was well after dark now. The streets were deserted.

Joe and I made the sharp left into the park entrance, tires squealing. We barreled along the main drive that wound through the park. I racked my brain, trying to remember where the steep sledding hill was.

We took the turns of the curving road at a speed that made me cringe. Each time I was convinced I'd skid out. Somehow I managed to stay upright. I gripped the handlebars so hard my knuckles were white. I wasn't sure I'd be able to peel them off when this horrible ride was over.

If I could walk away from it, that is.

Trees and fountains and statues and benches zipped by at an alarming clip. Didn't want to plow into any of those.

The hill appeared, and I really hoped Joe's idea would work. We zoomed up the hill, but I could definitely feel the bike having to work under me. At this point, slowing down even a little would be great!

I spotted a row of hedges near the crest. It seemed to be our only option. The bike would be working its hardest, and even though the hedges didn't exactly look comfy, they'd be a lot gentler than a tree.

"Go right!" I shouted.

I veered the bike toward the hedges. I shut my eyes, knowing my face below the helmet was going to get seriously scratched.

Impact! The bike made a strangled sound, and the branches grabbed at me. I didn't stop right away; the front shrubs pulled right out of the ground, and I continued for a few more feet. Once the bike had slowed down enough, I flung myself off.

Ooof! I landed hard, and whatever I landed on was not soft. I lay there a moment, doing an internal inventory. Bones in one piece? Check. Blood anywhere? Not as far as I could tell. Head still attached to my body? Check. Battered and bruised? Check and double check.

Slowly I got up into a sitting position. Man, the park landscapers were going to be seriously ticked off. Joe and I had taken out most of the hedges that lined the road, and we'd crushed the bushes we landed in. I saw Joe's blond head rise above the greenery and could tell he was also hurting, but safe.

And really, really angry.

"Why are they still trying to kill us?" he shouted. "We gave them the stupid PDA."

He stood and stomped over to his downed bike. He reached down and switched it off. If we had tried to just stop at that speed we would have gone flying over the bars and gone splat on the street. I knelt down beside mine and turned it off, too.

"Maybe the bikes had already been tampered with," I said. "Before Phillip's guys—I mean *Wong's* guys—got to us. They probably figure we know too much."

"I *know* this bike is going to need some pretty expensive repair," Joe fumed. "Can we send them the bill?"

I straightened back up. Man, I was sore. "I have a feeling we'd have a hard time collecting."

"Now what do we do?" Joe asked. "Our bikes are toast, we've done some major damage to this park, and we're still miles from home."

We looked at each other and simultaneously said, "Dad."

I pulled out my phone. "It's the only way to get this incident taken care of and past Mom."

Dad answered on the third ring. I quickly explained the sitch. As soon as he heard we were both okay, he promised to get to us ASAP, along with a tow for the bikes.

"Now we wait," I said, flipping the phone shut.

Joe paced back and forth, muttering.

"Care to share?" I ventured.

He threw up his hands. "This case just doesn't make sense. Nothing adds up!"

I nodded. "There are an awful lot of loose ends," I agreed. "And it's hard to stay on top of things if the players keep changing. We keep having to wrap our minds around new info, new motives, new everything."

"Yeah," Joe said. "Here's one. If Ryan was the 'insider,' why was Slick murdered?"

"Good point," I said. "I've got another. Where has Ryan been all this time? What if he never left at all and has been keeping an eye on things?"

Joe slowly turned to look at me. "Could Ryan

have killed Slick because he discovered the boot-legging scheme?"

I tugged on my lower lip. I sometimes do that when I'm trying to retrieve data from the back of my mental hard drive. There was something stored in there.

I got it. "Ryan's a black belt. Remember—he's the one who trained Justin for the movie!"

Joe's eyes widened as he put two and two together. "Slick was killed with a blow that a black belt could inflict. We thought it was the three goons. But it could have been Ryan!"

"Ryan is much more dangerous than we realized," I said.

Gone AWOL

I groaned as I rolled out of bed the next morning. Every muscle ached. I think they'd all seized up to protect my bones from the jarring emergency landing I'd made on the bike last night. Now they were letting me know how much work they had done on my behalf.

My skin hurt too—I had serious road rash.

But the worst thing was, there was no getting around Mom and Aunt Trudy. Dad had to let them know we were in an accident—how else to explain dashing out in the middle of the night? And our coming home beat up and minus the motorcycles?

We didn't want them thinking we'd been reckless

or we'd never be able to ride again. But we also didn't want them to know our brakes had been cut. Dad explained it by saying there was some kind of fluke malfunction with the bikes, so they were at the shop to make sure it didn't happen again.

Aunt T went off on how she always knew those bikes were trouble and that they were just an accident waiting to happen and how lucky we were that it wasn't worse.

I totally agreed with her on that last one. Someone wanted us dead, and we were very lucky that whoever it was didn't get his wish.

I was stretching, trying to work out some kinks, when Frank knocked on my door. I knew it was Frank because he always does an annoying little rhythm. Why can't he just knock? He doesn't have to go all percussive.

Okay, I was cranky. Not only had someone tried to off us—my beautiful bike was in the motorcycle hospital in intensive care! I was not in a good mood.

"Yeah, yeah, come on in," I said.

Frank opened the door. "Nice welcome," he said. He was carrying his laptop, so I had a feeling he had some info from ATAC.

That perked me up. I wanted to get this case solved once and for all. It was making me nuts!

"What do you have there?" I asked.

Frank put the computer on my desk and took a step back. "Pictures of guns from ATAC. They want to know if any of them look like that silver job Mr. Ninja used."

I sat on the desk chair. "They're all the right caliber?" I asked.

Frank nodded. "Based on the bullet we found on the roof. I spotted one I think it might be. I want to see if you pick the same one."

I scanned the images. There were four guns—all of them silver. But one stood out from the rest. I knew in my rattled bones I'd seen it before. The engraved handle, the small size, the shape of the nose. "That one," I said, pointing at it.

"I think so too," Frank said. "E-mail them and tell them."

I shot an e-mail to the ATAC secure site. In just a moment I got a reply:

That gun is an antique and rather rare. We'll investigate sales and get back to you.

Frank settled onto the floor. "Maybe we'll finally get somewhere," he said.

"I'm betting it was Wong," I said. "He had just seen us with the PDA, and those guys seemed awfully serious about getting it back."

"I don't know. . . ." Frank's eyes narrowed as he gave our suspects some thought. "When would Wong have had the time to change into that all-black gear and get the mask?"

"We had about a million courses at the restaurant," I pointed out. "He'd have plenty of time."

"The dude seemed bigger than Wong," Frank continued.

"So maybe it was a hit man working on Wong's call," I argued.

"But—"

My phone rang, which put an end to Frank's knocking down my theory. Good thing. In the mood I was in, I was ready to clock him.

"The smarter Hardy here," I said into the phone.

Frank raised an eyebrow and then shook his head.

"I'm so glad I got you!" Sydney Lamb blurted. She sounded really upset.

"What's wrong?" I asked, almost afraid of finding out the answer.

"First Ryan! Now Justin! Only it's so much worse that it's Justin!"

"Are you saying that Justin is gone?" I asked.

"He never showed up for his costume fitting this morning!" Sydney said. "Emily is worried sick because they were supposed to have breakfast and come to the set together, and he stood her up. At first she thought he was back to his old ways, but when she heard he didn't get to the trailer . . . well, you can imagine!"

I could. Not only did it mean shooting would have to shut down, costing them who knows how many hundreds of thousands of dollars, they were worried he'd done something really disastrous. Something Sydney couldn't get him out of.

I knew she was concerned about drugs, but I had a feeling that wasn't the problem, or why Justin was a no-show.

My guess? He'd gone to warn Ryan that we were onto him. Maybe help him disappear so completely the feds would never be able to track him.

"Frank and I will do our best to help find him," I promised, hoping I'd be able to make good on my word. "And tell Emily to be sure to keep her phone on. He might try to contact her."

"Let me know the minute you find out anything," Sydney said. "And I mean *anything*. Even if it's the kind of thing Justin wouldn't want me to know. I'm here for him."

"You got it."

"Justin's gone," Frank guessed when I turned around.

I nodded. "Sydney seems to be worried that he's overdosed or something."

"You don't think that," Frank said.

"I know we saw him taking those pills, and he may really be doing drugs, but I don't think that has anything to do with his disappearing act." I frowned. "Did Dad send off the pills for analysis?"

Frank nodded. "We'll know a lot more once we get that report."

"I hope so."

"You think Justin went to warn Ryan," said Frank.

"I do too."

"We have to figure out where Ryan is hiding," I said. "And fast. Or we may never find him again."

"With Justin's money, Ryan could get pretty much anywhere in the world. Hire a plane, bribe people, even get a fake passport."

"That all takes time," I reasoned. "That's a good thing. But we have to get some kind of clue to where Ryan might be. And so far, we've got nothing."

Frank's computer beeped, letting him know he had a new message. He turned to look at the screen. "It's from ATAC."

He opened the message and his jaw dropped.

"What?" I asked, crossing over to stand behind him. I peered at the screen.

An antique gun the same model as the one you saw was reported stolen recently. It was registered to someone named Ziziska.

"Ziziska!" I exclaimed. "That's Justin and Ryan's real last name!"

A Shot in the Dark

O nce again this case had taken an entirely bizarre new twist.

I hit REPLY and typed a question:

Walter Ziziska?

I got an answer right away.

No, Katherine Ziziska. She was once married to someone named Walter.

"Justin and Ryan's mother!" I exclaimed. "I have a hunch that the gun was stolen by one of her sons," Joe said. "And my money's on Ryan."

"Which means he's the guy who came after us in Chinatown," I said.

"You were right," Joe said. "It wasn't Wong or one of his men."

I swiveled around in my chair. "Did I just hear you correctly? Did you actually say I was right? Meaning you were wrong?"

"Hey, pay attention," Joe complained. "We have a case to handle."

"We never even asked about their mom," I realized.

"She wasn't mentioned in the court case when they were declared emancipated minors," said Joe. "I kinda assumed she was dead."

"Or maybe she was just dead to them, the way their dad was," I said.

"Hmm." Something occurred to me. I wrote another e-mail to ATAC:

When was it stolen?

The reply was:

Just a couple of weeks ago.

"If she had been dead to them, she's been resurrected," I said. "If Ryan was the one who took that gun, then he's been to her house. Recently."

"That could be his hideout. She's really off the tabloid radar."

"She's off *everyone's* radar," I said, after requesting her address from ATAC. "Most importantly, the tabloids. She's in a town I've never heard of in upstate New York."

"I say we pay Mama Ziziska a visit," said Joe. "She might not be willing to talk over the phone."

"Good idea. And even if Ryan isn't there, we may

WITNESS PROFILE

Name: Katherine Ziziska

Physical description: Late thirties, long blond hair, green eyes, 5'5", 130 lbs.

Background: Married just out of high school and had the twins right away. Moved to L.A. with Walter when the boys were infants. Hated L.A.—thought it was too commercial. Didn't think the boys should be in show biz. All this contributed to the divorce.

Member of a number of radical organizations— all against materialism, popular culture, and commercialism. Total hippie values.

Still in touch with both boys. Receives an

be able to pick up some clues by seeing the house. She might even have some idea where he'd go if he wanted to disappear."

I aked ATAC to find out all they could about Katherine Zizika, and then Joe and I worked up a witness profile.

"I don't get it," said Joe. "If she's so antimaterialistic, what's she doing being a collector? And taking money from Justin? She doesn't approve of the way he earns it."

"She must justify it all to herself somehow," I said. "People are awfully good at making their contradictions make sense."

"Nothing having to do with the Carraway twins—or the Ziziskas—has made any sense to me!" Joe said.

I called the mechanic and was deeply relieved to hear that the motorcycles were ready for pickup already. We knew Mom would object to our riding so soon after the accident, so we kind of snuck out without saying anything.

"Sweet!" Joe cheered as we hit the road. "This baby rides even smoother than it did before."

"That's good," I told him. "We're going to be riding for a few hours."

We made good time. It was a weekday, and we had missed the rush-hour traffic. After a couple of hours, we pulled up to a roadside diner for a pit stop. We scarfed down some sandwiches, and then I checked in with one of our usual contacts at ATAC.

"Any new info we should know about?" I asked.

"We just got back the results from the lab on that pill you sent us. I was just about to call you."

I braced myself for the worst. "So what kind of drugs are they?" I asked.

"Nothing special. Prescription allergy pills."

"Really?" I asked.

"We ran it twice. So the good news is, Justin isn't taking drugs. Well, he is, just not the kind you were worried about."

"Thanks," I said.

I hung up and stared at the phone.

"What?" Joe asked. "You look like that phone is an alien creature."

"Huh?" I looked up. "Just got some news. Good news, I guess." But if that was true, why did I find the news so unsettling? I tried to shake off the feeling. "They got the drug analysis back. Those pills aren't anything more serious than allergy pills."

Now Joe looked puzzled. "So we were wrong. And Sydney doesn't have to worry. That's good." But he sounded as uncertain as I felt.

"Then why do I feel like we just got hit with a whammy?"

Joe frowned. Then his eyes widened. "Because Justin doesn't have allergies," he exclaimed. "Ryan does!"

Double Deception

I t all slammed into place. "Ryan has taken over as Justin!" I said. "It explains everything! His weird behavior, his less-than-stellar acting in the movie, even not knowing the high rollers in Atlantic City."

"It especially explains the change in the Justin–Emily romance," Frank said. "Ryan had a big crush on her."

"So Ryan finally got the girl," I said.

"Yeah, by pretending to be someone else."

"How did he get away with it?"

"He started out as an actor, remember? And in Atlantic City he spent more time with us than with people who knew him a whole lot better."

"How did he get Justin to go along with it?" I asked. "How did he keep him quiet?"

Frank frowned. "He must have had something to blackmail Justin with."

I had another *aha!* moment. "What if Justin really *had* been the 'insider,' as we first thought? Ryan could have found out and used that to get Justin out of the picture."

"But what was Ryan's ultimate plan? Did he really think Justin would have allowed it to go on forever? Did Ryan think no one would ever find out?"

"We'll know more once we confront the twins," I said. "Whichever one we find first."

"The hard part is knowing which twin we're actually talking to."

We climbed back aboard the bikes. I was glad we didn't have much farther to go. My body was still hurting from last night's adventure.

The route became more and more rural. After about an hour we pulled up to a small white house with blue shutters. The front lawn was overgrown with weeds and wildflowers. Instead of a backyard, there were miles of woods behind the house. We had passed the last house about ten miles back.

"If she doesn't want to be found, this is a good place to be," I said.

"Same thing goes for Ryan," said Frank.

We parked the bikes at the side of the road. "You know what we haven't figured out?" I said. "Where has Justin been all this time?"

"Maybe here," Frank suggested.

"Do we have a cover story?" I asked. "Or do we just go in and ask where the twins are?"

Frank reached for the doorbell. "Time is running out," he said. "I guess we should just be direct."

The doorbell chimed, and a moment later a woman appeared behind the screen. She wore a loose floral dress, and her long hair was piled up on top of her head. "Yes?" she said, looking puzzled.

"Excuse me, Ms. Ziziska, we're friends of your sons," Frank said.

She frowned. "Okay . . ." She looked confused.

"We've been on the road for a while," I said. I pointed to our bikes. If she was such a hippie, she might be into motorcycles. "We knew where you lived because Ryan and Justin told us, and we could really use a drink of water and maybe use your bathroom."

She peered through the screen at the bikes. "Nice rides," she said. She smiled and opened the door. "Come on in."

We walked into the small house. My nose wrinkled. I was trying to figure out what was causing the foul smell when I realized there were about ten cats loung-ing around.

"Hope you boys aren't allergic," she said, step-ping over a fat orange tabby.

"No, ma'am," said Frank.

"Please!" she said with a laugh. "Ma'am makes me sound so old! Call me Katie."

"Sure thing, Katie," I said. "You don't look old enough to have teenage sons."

It was true—and I could see that the boys took after her a lot more than they did their dad. She was attractive now and had probably been a smokin' teen.

Frank stepped up to a glass case. "You collect antique guns?" he asked.

"Not for shooting, of course!" she said. "I'm a complete pacifist. I don't even kill flies."

She stepped up to the case. "But they're awfully pretty. And each one has a history. It's why I like antiques. First of all, you're not buying into the cheap commercialism of our disposable consumer society. Second—"

I stopped her before she went on a soapbox rant. "Looks like there's one missing."

She frowned. "I don't know what happened. It just disappeared." She bent down and picked up a gray kitten that was rubbing against her leg. "Did you take it, Smokey?" she cooed to the kitten. "Did you?"

I glanced around looking for some kind of clue that would help us figure out where Ryan was—and what his next move would be.

My eyes landed on a little blue cell phone. Just like the one I'd seen in Justin's trailer.

That's why the call had come from Ryan's cell—he was using his own when he called Phillip, trying to figure out if he was dead or alive. He must have used Justin's to call people he was trying to convince he was Justin. Caller ID can really trip up a crime!

"Where are the guys?" I said. "We'd love to see them."

Katie put the little cat down. "How would I know?" she said. "I haven't seen them in years." Then her eyes narrowed, and she glared at me. "Wouldn't you know that if you were friends."

"Actually, we're such good friends we know that's not true," Frank said.

I waited to see how she'd handle that bait. She looked puzzled, then said, "I don't have all day. Do you want some water or not?" Her face grew angry again. "Or did you just come here trying to find out something about the boys?"

"No, no," I assured her, giving Frank an raised eyebrow that pleaded for help. "Water is definitely our goal here."

"And the bathroom," Frank added.

"Especially the bathroom," I stressed. This would give us an excuse to go through the house.

She still studied us suspiciously.

"After we take care of . . . business," I said, "you want a ride? You look like you'd know your way around a bike."

Katie's expression softened. "You bet! I'll get you some water. Or would you prefer some nice iced herbal tea? I could make up a batch in a jiff."

"Tea is perfect," said Frank.

It sure was. That "jiff" would give us valuable searching time.

"Ooh," Katie said. "I think I still have some great granola carob cookies to go with it." She vanished into the kitchen.

"Quick," Frank whispered. "Let's see if we can find anything in the bedrooms that will help us."

We hurried down the hall. The first door we opened was Katie's bedroom—it was full of more of those loose, colorful dresses and weird art on the walls. The next door was another bedroom.

"Looks like a guest room," Frank commented. "Nothing really personal, but functional."

I ducked down to look under the bed. I dragged out a pair of expensive sneakers. Not Katie's size. "It's been functioning, all right."

"There are papers on that desk by the window," said Frank. "You look through those while I check out the closet."

I stepped over to the desk, and my eyes bugged.

"Whoa!" I said. "Come take a look at this!"

I lifted up the note for Frank to see.

He gasped. "It's a suicide note. Signed by Ryan. Confessing to the bootlegging scheme. And Slick's murder."

"It's just like Justin said," I exclaimed. "He worried that if Ryan's involvement in the bootleg business came out, Ryan would do something desperate."

Frank looked grim. "You're forgetting something. It wasn't Justin who said that. It was Ryan, *pretending* to be Justin!"

"But why . . ." Then I smacked my forehead. "This is Ryan's way out!"

"Exactly." Frank nodded. "The *real* Ryan is going to kill the *real* Justin and make it look like suicide. He'll claim it was Ryan who died."

"He'll blame everything on Ryan, go scot-free, and play the role of Justin for the rest of his life," I said. "It's an amazing plan."

"It also means that time is running out for the real Justin."

Twisted Twins

"**W**e have to find Justin and Ryan. Now," Joe said.

"Justin—I mean, Real Ryan—didn't have that much of a head start," I said. "The phone is still here. I'm betting they're still nearby."

I paced back and forth in front of the little desk. I glanced out the window. I snapped my fingers. "The woods!"

Joe raced over to the window and looked out. "If I was going to get rid of someone, that would be a smart place to do it. Anyone hearing a gunshot would probably think it was a hunter."

"And it would take a long time to find the body," I added. "Giving Ryan—the real Ryan—a chance to get away, create an alibi, and go back to being Justin."

"For the rest of his life."

I slipped the fake suicide note into my pocket. It was evidence, but I also didn't want Ms. Ziziska to find it and have a meltdown. Especially since Joe and I were going to do everything we could to prevent this murder.

"Boys?" Katie Ziziska called. "The tea is ready!" I heard her coming down the hall. "Where are you?"

An edge had crept into her voice, and I had a feeling she was back to suspecting us of something. We couldn't let her slow us down.

I yanked back the curtains and shoved the window open. I swung my leg over. "Hate to be this rude, but—"

"A guy's gotta do what a guy's gotta do," Joe finished for me.

We landed and ran straight for the woods. Once we were no longer visible from the house, we slowed down. We needed to move carefully and quietly. We didn't want to alert Ryan.

"He's a lot crazier than we ever realized," Joe said.

"Or a lot more desperate," I replied.

"Which way do you think he went?" Joe asked.

"Do you see any signs of life?"

We both knelt down, trying to see if there were

any clues to follow. The trees blocked a lot of the sunlight. I wished we'd brought flashlights.

Joe had moved away from me. "I think I found something."

I joined him. "Looks like a path."

"A path taken by six-foot-tall blondes."

I gaped at him. "How do you get that?"

Joe smirked. "The powers of observation." He pulled a branch toward me. "See? Strand of blond hair at just about our height."

I whistled in admiration. "You may be cut out for this line of work after all."

Joe rolled his eyes. "*Anyway*. I figure they got onto the path here."

"Let's travel parallel, then. We don't want them to notice us before we notice them."

We crept into the brush alongside the path and moved deeper into the trees. We were still able to see where the path went, but it would be pretty hard to see us.

We moved slowly, stepping over thick roots and ducking under branches. We hadn't gone very far when I heard voices. I motioned for Joe to stop.

"Please, Ryan, no," I heard someone begging. "I'll give you anything you want!"

We had found them. It sounded as if Justin was pleading for his life.

I snuck closer and peered through the branches into a clearing. My stomach twisted.

Justin was kneeling on the ground, with his hands tied behind his back. Ryan pointed the antique gun at him.

"I've got it all anyway!" Ryan said. "And I need to put an end to this. Right now!"

Oh no, you won't, I thought. I flung myself out of my hiding place and raced to Ryan. He whirled, but I was ready for him. I slammed into the arm holding the gun with my elbow. The gun went flying, and Ryan stumbled backward.

Joe raced after the gun. "It landed in a stream!" he shouted, then jogged back over to us.

I was feeling confident. There were two Hardys and only one dangerous Carraway. "I don't get it," I said. "What was the point of all of this, Ryan?"

"It's not about the money, is it?" asked Joe.

"Of course not," Ryan sneered.

"Then what?" Justin begged. I could see how destroyed he was. His own twin wanted him dead.

"I was going to prove I'm a better Justin than you!" Ryan snapped at Justin. He turned to us. "I'd be more professional. I'd be nicer. And I'd be just as good in the movie."

"But you weren't, remember?" I said. "The director wasn't happy." Harsh, I know, but I wanted to get him to lose his cool. He'd be easier to over-power. I wasn't forgetting for a minute that he was a black belt—and capable of murder.

"Th-that's why you did it?" Justin asked. "To show me up?"

"I'd get the career you have!" Ryan answered. "But it was so much more complicated than I thought it would be."

I began putting the pieces together. "You didn't know that your brother still owed money to Phillip Yu, did you?"

Ryan shook his head. "I knew about Justin's stupid bootlegging. That's how I got him to go along with the plan. I was just going to do it for a little while. I told him I'd erase all the evidence."

"Yeah, that was after you already threatened to expose me," Justin retorted.

Joe stepped in front of Justin. I knew he didn't want Ryan to go after Justin—the guy was still tied up and totally helpless. "That's why you were so scared when you thought Phillip might still be alive," Joe said. "And why you freaked when you found out we had all the info from his PDA."

I started circling around so that Joe and I had Ryan in between us. "You tampered with our bikes. You went after us in Chinatown."

"It was all falling apart," Ryan moaned. "Just when

things were going so great with Emily!"

"That was when you decided to stay Justin forever, wasn't it?" Joe said. "Because of Emily."

"This was about *Emily*?" said Justin. "Dude! I had zero interest in her! You could have had her without doing all this!"

"She was never interested in me!" Ryan shouted. "Only you!"

"Besides, you liked all that went with being the movie star," I said. "It wasn't just Emily. It was all of it."

"It should have been mine. Slick had no right to take it all away from me!"

"Is that why you killed him?" Joe demanded. "As revenge?"

Justin slumped. "Slick is dead?" he asked, his voice breaking.

"He was on to me. He found out about Justin's bootlegging, and when he confronted me, he realized I wasn't Justin. He knew it was me. I had to kill him."

"I had no idea you were this crazy," Justin said.

"I didn't start out this way!" Ryan snapped. "You all made me this way!"

"And Elijah Gorman? The photographer?" I asked. That first murder had nagged at me ever since we couldn't tie it to Justin's stalker.

"Elijah." Ryan practically spat his name. "Bottom-feeder."

"You didn't kill him because you objected to his journalist practices," Joe said. "So why did you?"

"He was there when I confronted Justin about the bootlegging scheme. He recorded it on his cell and took photos of us arguing. It would have revealed everything—and he just couldn't wait to expose us."

He turned to face me. "Just like you and your brother!"

Without warning, he charged me. He moved so quickly I barely registered the attack until his foot connected with my stomach.

"Oof!" I doubled over, clutching my gut. After last night's motorcycle near crash, I was sore all over. This was not going to help!

I could see Joe chasing Ryan. I forced myself back up and ran after them. Joe was in great shape, but he was no match for a black belt like Ryan.

Not alone, anyway.

Joe flung himself onto Ryan's back, and they fell to the ground. They rolled around together and I couldn't tell who had the upper hand. It didn't matter—I was going in.

Ryan managed to flip Joe off and was scrambling to get back on his feet. I slammed into him, knocking him back to the ground. He kicked out hard, connecting painfully with my shin. I stumbled, but Joe was on it. As Ryan raised his arm to slug me, Joe surprised him and grabbed it.

Ryan spun around and slammed Joe in the side of the head.

That had to hurt. But Joe never let go. That gave me time to grab Ryan's other arm.

"Let go of me!" he shouted.

He tried to use his powerful kick, but it only made him lose his balance.

"We need to tie him up," said Joe.

"Justin's restraints!" I exclaimed.

We dragged the squirming, squalling, screaming Ryan over to his twin. We lowered him to the ground. I still gripped his arm, and Joe sat on him. He quickly untied Justin and then lashed the rope around Ryan's wrists. Then I pulled off my belt and wrapped that around his legs. I wasn't taking any chances.

"I—I don't know how to thank you guys," Justin said, rubbing his wrists. His face was ashen, and he looked like he was trying not to cry.

"It's not over yet," I told him. "The authorities already know about your role in the bootlegging operation. That's a crime."

He nodded. "What's going to happen to my brother?"

"I don't know," I answered honestly. "He obviously needs help. And after all this, I'm guessing you do too."

"I just never imagined . . . I never thought. . . ." Justin's voice choked up, and he couldn't continue.

I felt for the guy. I may tell Joe I want to kill him, but I'd never actually do it. It must be unreal to know your own twin had it in for you.

"Cops are on their way," Joe said, slipping his phone into his pocket. "Dispatch said a squad car was in the area already."

I heard sirens not too far off, and then some crashing in the woods.

"Over here!" I called.

Two uniformed officers emerged from the trees. We explained as much as we could and watched Justin and Ryan being handcuffed and led away.

I slung my belt back through the loops. "That's really sad," I commented. "Justin had no idea how much Ryan hated him."

"I think it's sadder how far Ryan was willing to go," Joe said. "His envy really and truly made him crazy."

We started to walk the path to get out of the woods and back to our bikes. "Oh, man," I said. "You know who's going to be really torn up about Justin going to jail? Aunt Trudy!"

Joe laughed. "You're right!"

"We'd better not let her know we had anything to do with ending his career," I said.

Joe looked at me and grinned. "Ended it for now, anyway. Probably not forever. What did that producer say? Everyone loves a bad boy!"

Here's a sneak peek at the first adventure in the
GALAXY X TRILOGY,
#28: *GALAXY X*

FRANK

Diving In

"**H**ang on!" I shouted.

Acting on instinct, I raced to the edge of the pool and dove in. Luckily, the girl was only a few yards from the edge of the pool where Joe and I had been sitting. I reached her in about three strokes.

She stopped thrashing when I got there. I grabbed her under the arms, making sure her head stayed above water.

"Just relax," I said. "I've got you."

She sort of gurgled and nodded. Her body relaxed, allowing me to drag her along with me.

I turned and struck out for dry land, holding on to the girl with one arm and swimming with the other. By the time we reached the edge of the pool, a small crowd had gathered.

"It's okay," Joe was saying to the onlookers. "My brother is trained in water rescue."

That was true. Both of us had taken a course when we'd signed on with ATAC. We'd also learned a bunch of other cool stuff, from rappelling to judo.

"Hey, what's going on?" The lifeguard on duty pushed his way forward.

I grimaced. Said lifeguard was Brian Conrad. He's this guy we know from school. I'd been a little surprised to show up at the pool and see that he'd landed a job as lifeguard. He normally isn't the helping-people type. Or the holding-down-a-job type, for that matter.

"Can you grab the edge?" I asked the girl, ignoring Brian.

She nodded and reached for the edge of the pool. "Thanks, I'm okay now," she said. "I can get out myself."

"No, hang on, I'll help you." Joe was already reaching for her hands.

"Hey, back off, amateurs." Brian had reached us. "Pulling people out of the pool is my job."

Joe shot him a look. "If we had to wait for you to actually do *your* job, she'd be at the bottom of the pool right now."

"Whatever. Come on, babe." Brian reached for the girl.

She shook off his hand. "I'm fine," she said coolly, hoisting herself out of the pool in one graceful motion.

She was amazing-looking. I tried not to stare.

Joe wasn't even trying. His eyes were practically bulging out of his head.

The girl turned to me, still ignoring Brian. "Thank you so much for coming to my rescue," she said, putting a hand on my arm.

"That's my brother." Joe shouldered past Brian to get closer to the girl. "He's a real hero. We have a lot in common that way. How about if you sit down and catch your breath, and I'll tell you all about it?"

"Forget it, Joe Hardhead," Brian said. "This girl needs medical attention. I'll take over from here."

The girl gave him an icy look. "I already said I'm fine. I don't need a doctor."

Before Brian could respond, she took me by the arm and dragged me after her. Joe followed. Most of the other onlookers drifted away, the excitement over.

I glanced back over my shoulder at Brian. He was sort of gritting his teeth. He took a few steps after us. But just then a big, beefy-looking guy in his twenties appeared. He was wearing swim trunks and a whistle.

"Yo, Conrad," he barked. "Why aren't you at your post?" He pointed to the empty lifeguard stand.

Joe snorted with laughter as Brian started to whine excuses at his boss. "Nice," he commented. "Wonder how long Brian's going to last at this job?"

The girl didn't seem interested in any of that. She dropped my arm as we reached a lounge chair with a flowered bag on it. Reaching into the bag, she pulled out a large hardcover book.

"I wish I had something better to give you to show my thanks. But this will have to do." With that, she shoved the book into my hands.

I glanced down at it. It looked like some kind of sweeping historical novel. Not really my thing—not that I was about to tell her that.

"Um, thanks," I said. "But it was really no big…"

My voice trailed off. She'd just grabbed the bag off the chair and rushed away. "Be sure to read that book, okay?" she called back over her shoulder. "Do it for me!"

"Hey!" Joe called after her. "Come back. You didn't even tell us your name."

"Give it up, Joe," I said as the girl disappeared around the corner. "If you wanted her number, you missed your chance."

He frowned. "Maybe her name and number are written inside the book," he suggested. "She seemed pretty eager for you to read it."

The guy never gives up hope. Mostly just to appease him, I flipped open the cover. My eyes widened immediately, and I slammed the book shut again.

"What?" Joe asked.

I tucked the book carefully under my arm. "Come on," I told him. "I think we'd better head home."

"As soon as I opened that book and saw the DVD stuck inside, I figured we'd just received our next mission," I commented as I sat down in front of the video game console on my desk.

Joe and I were in my bedroom at home. We'd rushed back from the pool to find the house empty. Aunt Trudy was weeding the flower garden out back, but we'd sneaked past without letting her know we were home. Sometimes that was easier than answering her questions. Okay, make that *most* of the time.

Joe shook his head as he flopped onto the end of my bed. "I can't believe that girl was an ATAC agent," he said. "Dude, why can't *she* be my partner instead of you?"

Ignoring him, I slid the DVD out of the book.

The label made it look like a concert video from the latest Mr. Nice Guyz tour. All our ATAC assignments come on CDs or DVDs. One play is all we get to take in the details of our next assignment. After that, they revert to whatever's on the label—movie, music, video game, whatever. So it's key to pay attention the first time.

Paying attention isn't always Joe's strong suit, so I glanced back at him. "Ready?" I asked, my finger poised over the START button.

"Let's do it." He sat up and leaned forward. "And let's hope that it isn't another girly assignment."

The DVD began with the usual welcome from our ATAC boss, who went by the name Q. After that, the briefing started.

"Welcome to a whole new galaxy of action and excitement," a voice intoned to a background of wailing guitar-heavy music. The picture on the screen jumped to a shot of a hilly, brushy outdoor track of some sort. Several mountain bikes raced past, jumping and skidding along the track. Then the shot jumped to a steep, icy mountain, with several skiers whooshing past at top speed. After that, the scene shifted again, this time to crashing waves with surfers riding in on longboards.

"Awesome!" Joe blurted out, his eyes glued to the screen.

"Still worried it's going to be a girly assignment?" I joked.

Then I shut up, because the voice was speaking again. *"Welcome to Galaxy X,"* it said. *"A brand-new theme park certain to be a dream destination for anyone who craves some radical excitement in their lives."*

"Whoa, Galaxy X? I've heard about that place," Joe said. "It's being built on some island off the Carolina coast, right?"

I nodded. "I've heard of it too. It's supposed to be the brainchild of Tyrone McKenzie."

"The music producer?"

"Uh-huh." I'd just read a story about McKenzie and his pet project in a news magazine. Hitting PAUSE, I searched my mind for the details. "The place is supposed to be a dream come true for teenage boys. There are regular theme-park-type attractions like roller coasters and stuff, but it goes way beyond that."

"I know!" Joe put in. "I saw a whole story about it on TV last week. There's going to be a huge BMX track, rock-climbing walls, a totally cool skateboard park, a wave pool, cliff diving, street luge, snowboarding . . ."

"Sounds like fun." I pressed the button to start the recording again.

The announcer told us pretty much everything

we'd just discussed. Basically, Galaxy X was going to be a testosterone paradise. In addition to the X Game–type stuff and the roller coasters, there would be a huge arcade, tons of food, awesome 3-D movies, and lots more.

"Sounds like fun, right?" the voice on the DVD said. *"Well, apparently somebody doesn't think so. Tyrone McKenzie has been receiving threats from someone who doesn't want Galaxy X to open at all. When these threats were limited to e-mail and blogs, Mr. McKenzie wasn't concerned. However, recently there has been some graffiti and other vandalism at the site itself, and with the grand opening approaching, he called the authorities. And that's where you come in. . . ."*

"Yes!" Joe jumped to his feet and pumped both fists in the air. "Galaxy X, here we come!"

"Hang on," I cautioned him. "We don't want to miss the rest of the message."

But there wasn't much after that. The announcer explained that Joe and I would be heading down to Galaxy X immediately, arriving just before the start of something Tyrone McKenzie was calling "Preview Daze." That was when the park would be open only to various young, hip celebrities, reviewers, and other media types. Joe and I would be posing as radio contest winners who'd scored tickets to the preview. We were supposed to blend in and investigate—find out if there was any real danger behind the threats.

Finally Q reappeared onscreen. *"Be careful, agents,"* he warned in his usual super-serious way. Then he shot the camera a quick "hang loose" sign with one hand and cracked a smile. *"And have fun."*

With that, the screen went black. "Wow, this is great," Joe said, hopping around the room like the ball in a pinball machine. "This has to be the greatest mission ever!"

"Not exactly," I said. "Based on what we just heard, we don't even know what we're supposed to be looking for."

Joe shrugged. "So what? That's nothing new—our missions are usually mysterious like that. Look at the big picture, man. Even if this McKenzie dude is being totally paranoid and it's just a few disgruntled bloggers behind the trouble, we still end up with a few free days of hanging out with celebs and having an awesome time testing out all those cool attractions before the place even opens to the public." He grinned and lifted one hand. "And here we thought we'd be stuck here and bored for the rest of our summer vacation!"

I couldn't help grinning back and giving him a high five. "Okay, maybe you're right," I admitted. "It definitely beats ballet."

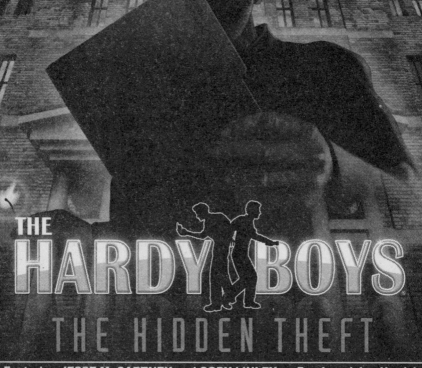